CHAOS LIES BENEATH THE NIGHT

EPISODE 1: GIFTS

J. LEIGH BRALICK

VORONA BOOKS

2023 Vorona Books Edition.

Copyright © 2021 by J. Leigh Bralick

Originally published in the United States by SisterMuses in 2021.

Published by Vorona Books, the publishing division of Vorona, LLC, Texas.
580 Decker Dr, Suite 105, Irving, TX 75062

ISBN: 9781941108277 (Paperback)| ISBN: 9781941108260 (eBook) | ISBN: 9781941108284 (Audiobook)

Cover and book design by Jennifer Lee

In loving memory of Nancy Bralick

With special thanks to Geni and James

Vignette

Arkastel — City of Taris

25 years ago

A BLANKET OF INCENSE SMOTHERED THE AIR INSIDE THE SANCTUARY of the High Fane, the smoke making wraiths of the red and blue light that slipped in through the colored-glass windows. Ingmar ven Karda shifted his weight from one foot to the other, trying desperately not to sneeze as the black-cowled thurifer swung his bronze censer again. Beside him, his fellow acolyte coughed quietly into the sleeve of his green robe. Ingmar wondered if age gave immunity to the tickling odor, because even when the cloud of smoke blossomed over them, none of the fully-initiated theomancers so much as twitched.

All five of them stood in a ring, silent, rigid beneath a gnawing anticipation, before the black stone slab that served as the Fane's altar. Besides the thurifer in his sepulchral robe, all were impressively dressed for the invocation, their ceremonial cloaks beaded and threaded in gold, their wrists twined, symbolically, with silver-sheened chains. Heaped on the altar were gifts fitting for a god—jewels, fine cloth, bottles of the rarest liquors in all the world, exotic perfumes in gilded vials.

Ingmar had barely glanced at the treasure. Despite his best intentions, his attention was held captive by the greatest offering the theomancers had for the Shadow Lord of Nyfalla—a young woman, no more than five years older than himself, caged in by the theomancers' ring.

Her dark hair had been ornately styled on the crown of her head, and she was dressed in a simple robe the color of blood. Ingmar's fellow acolyte, Palimo, believed that when the *Skaed* came to claim the girl, she would be killed in ritual offering, and that was why she was dressed all in red. Her hands were bound with scarlet silk, but Ingmar doubted they served any purpose; he'd seen her eyes when they brought her into the Temple, wide and staring, irises swallowed by the yawn of her pupils, drug-slack and uncaring.

Ingmar hadn't argued with Palimo's conviction; the other boy surely knew more than he did about it. Although they were both sixteen, Palimo had lived at the Fane since shortly after his birth, and knew far more than Ingmar about the rituals and the Aetherial beings they worshiped. Neither had ever witnessed an actual cabal, but Palimo stood stalwart with ancient patience as though he'd witnessed a hundred.

Ingmar could barely suppress his own nervous excitement. He twisted his hands in the folds of his robe and blinked again against the stinging smoke. For the last four years he had been studying the Aetherials of Light and Shadow under

Brother Garrim's tutelage, but he had never seen one become incarnate. He had never even seen a painting or depiction of one—a sacrilege that merited fire, and a cold and unmarked grave. What would a Nyfallan look like? A monstrous, hideous creature only vaguely resembling a human? An animal? A knot of shadow merely stirring the incense haze? He could hardly imagine.

Sister Resida stepped up to the middle of the altar and lifted her hands, making the beaded lengths of her cloak glimmer like falling embers.

"*Skaed* Morayn, come and hear our pleas!" she called out, her low voice echoing eerily between the temple's stone walls. "Claim the offerings we have prepared for your divine enjoyment. Do not scorn our miserable state but bless us with your presence!"

A prickle, spider quick and cold, chased over Ingmar's skin. He shot a nervous glance at Palimo, whose crooked teeth flashed as he grinned back at him. This was it. At any moment, the Prince of Shadow would materialize out of the air to hear the cabal. What would he say? Would he even listen to the theomancers' plea for mercy?

A faint metallic noise filtered through the emptiness above Ingmar's head. Of one accord, the two theomancers who held candles blew them out, and shadow descended over them. In all the temple, the only light that remained were the muted red and blue ribbons of daylight trickling, purple-dark, from the high windows. All the theomancers by the altar dropped to their knees and lifted up their hands; it looked like a gesture of surrender. Palimo jerked on Ingmar's sleeve and Ingmar stumbled to his knees beside the other boy. The girl in the blood red dress seemed to lift her chin, but made no other movement—was it cruelty or kindness that she not feel fear in this moment?

After a moment, Ingmar blinked frantically. His vision was blurring strangely…or no, not his vision but the air itself, wavering like a heat mirage. And then, between one breath and the next, a man stood before the theomancers. Ingmar swallowed hard. That was no monster—that was the most beautiful person he had ever seen. He looked barely a day older than Ingmar. His hair, straight and long, hung below his shoulders, shimmering like shadowed quicksilver. His elegant figure was perfectly accentuated by a fitted coat wrought in scarlet and charcoal silk, embroidered throughout with silver thread in whimsical lines, star-patterns, weighted with meaning Ingmar couldn't fathom. And he stared at the theomancers through the coldest, cruelest silver eyes Ingmar had ever seen.

If he hadn't just materialized out of sheer nothingness, Ingmar never would have known he was an Aetherial.

"You presume to ask us for favors?" he asked.

Ingmar shivered involuntarily. That voice was like silk, or ice—a veneer of calm barely veiling disgust.

Sister Resida lifted her hands a little higher and bowed her head. "*Skaed* Morayn—"

"I am not the *Skaed*," the Nyfallan snapped. "Do you imagine my prince would waste his time coming in person to hear whatever requests you have the audacity to make?"

Ingmar swallowed hard and glanced again at Palimo,

but the boy was staring wide-eyed at the Nyfallan and didn't notice. All the other theomancers were bowed low over their knees, leaving Resida alone to face the Nyfallan's displeasure.

"Do you speak for the *Skaed*?" she asked.

"No one speaks for the *Skaed* but the *Skaed* himself," said the Nyfallan. "But I will take your message to him, if I believe it is worth the effort."

Resida lowered her arms and got to her feet. She was a tiny woman, frail even before the unkindness of age, and in front of the tall Nyfallan she looked like a child. But she faced the Aetherial with more boldness than Ingmar would have expected.

"My lord, honored Nyfallan," she said, "please beseech your *Skaed* to have pity on us. Your Guards are harassing our people, terrifying them in their effort to maintain order on our streets. We hear reports on a near-daily basis of citizens found soul-devoured, which your prince promised would never happen, except—" Her voice cut off abruptly, and an odd silence followed that Ingmar did not understand at all. Then she shook her head faintly and finished, "Our people have grown afraid of even venturing outside at night, lest they inadvertently attract unwanted attention from your patrols."

A faint smirk fractured the perfection of the Nyfallan's face. "Rumors," he said. "Hearsay. Where is your evidence of wrongdoing? Which Guards are guilty of these transgressions? And that other accusation you have made." He paused, and Ingmar could have sworn the shadows grew darker all around him, like a gathering storm, heavy, laced with hectic energy. "You are bold to speak so glibly, when you know full well what you are claiming."

Ingmar tried to catch Palimo's attention, his curiosity raging at fever-pitch, but the other boy ignored him. Gritting his teeth, Ingmar looked back at the altar, his gaze fixed on Resida because he didn't have the courage to look on the Nyfallan. He didn't need to be a full theomancer to realize that this meeting was not going well at all; a sheep's interrogation of its butcher would have been more hopeful. But Resida was one of the strongest women he had ever known—not that he had known many women in his short life. She had to be afraid, but she gave no sign of it.

"I am sorry, lord. I do not have names," she said, then added, firmly, "I doubt the victims of these terrors thought to ask their attackers what their names were."

That brought a genuine grin to the Nyfallan's face, and he tipped his head in a nod, acknowledging the point. "Indeed," he said. "And I doubt it is every single Nyfallan Guard who is guilty of these imagined crimes. I will advise the *Skaed* to instruct his Guards to be more...gentle...with your fragile people."

He took a step forward, but halted just before he came under one of the gloomy ribbons of light. Ingmar might have imagined it, but he could have sworn a grimace of pain flickered across the Nyfallan's face.

The Shadow went on, "But perhaps you should ask your ruler to take care of his own. If you dislike how we conduct our affairs, it would be better if your own people keep out of our way. You know how we work. Tell them to stay in after dark. What could be simpler? It would make our Guards' job easier to do without your people in our way. Never forget, mortal—we send our people to your streets out of *mercy*. What we do is for your protection. Do not presume to question our methods."

"My lord, the Pyrion Guards have no trouble doing *their* job without harassing us! They work among us by daylight and we scarcely notice their presence. Don't tell me your Guards are less capable than they are."

"Resida!" hissed Brother Garrim, but his warning came too late.

Without a word, his face as calm as ever, the Nyfallan stretched out his flawless hand toward Resida. An anguished scream lacerated the temple's silence, and Ingmar watched, transfixed with horror, as Resida's skin turned an ashen grey. Her body went rigid, then, without another sound, she dropped to her knees with a bitter crack.

"Did you *kill* her?" Garrim cried, starting forward.

The Nyfallan swung his head to stare at him, and Garrim stopped short. "Do not try me, priest," the Aetherial spat. "Do not presume to judge above your nature." He jerked his chin at Resida. "She is not dead. But she might as well be. Do not consider it a kindness that I didn't kill her. I leave her with you as a warning."

His gaze shifted to the girl standing unmoved in the midst of the theomancers.

"Did you…did you eat her soul?" Ingmar gasped, before he could cage in the words.

Both acolytes had been strictly admonished to make

themselves invisible for the invocation. Ingmar's heart thudded painfully against his ribs as the Nyfallan's eyes turned toward him, and he realized he was very, very visible. Pinned by the Nyfallan's frigid stare, Ingmar prayed he would just die quickly. Anything to be free of the weight of his attention.

"No."

The word cut the silence like a shard of ice. Ingmar held his breath, unable to look away from the Shadow's silver eyes, and waited for the inevitable moment that he would share Resida's fate.

Then the Nyfallan looked away.

Ingmar swayed on his knees. Palimo's hand darted out, subtly, and caught his elbow.

"Will you intercede with the *Skaed* for us?" Brother Havlor whispered.

"Take care of your own house," said the Nyfallan. "I will consider it, but I make you no promises." He pointed at the girl. "I will take that. She is Shadow-marked, and the *Skaed*'s rightful property. You have no authority to withhold her, to use her as a hostage to bribe the *Skaed*, as if he owes you anything." He glanced back at the altar. "The rest is worthless."

As he gestured to the pile of treasure, all the light and color seemed to drain away from the cloth and baubles, leaving them grey as bones, empty husks. Then, without another word, he stepped around the pool of red light and strode toward the theomancers. Ingmar wondered if they might hold fast, but at his approach they relaxed their protective circle around the girl. The Nyfallan, not even sparing them a glance, took the girl by the elbow and vanished.

For endless moments after he had gone, no one in the temple moved. Then, with a broken sob, Brother Garrim darted to Resida's side and grasped her shoulders. She slumped into his arms like a rag doll. Of one accord, Ingmar and Palimo rushed forward to join the theomancers. Ingmar couldn't breathe; he could hear nothing but the hammering of his own pulse in his ears.

"What's wrong with her?" asked Havlor, kneeling beside Garrim.

"I don't know!" Garrim cried. He lifted his face to look at them, his cheeks streaked with tears. "Look at her. She's... she's just *gone*. But she's alive. Oh gods, what have we done to deserve this?"

"We must pray, brothers," Havlor said. "Pray the Nyfallan will bring our plea to the *Skaed*. We have no other hope."

"What will we tell the city was the outcome of the cabal?" one of the other priests asked. He was staring, rigid with fear, at the skeleton of offerings heaped on the altar.

Garrim, still cradling Resida in his arms, said nothing.

After a moment Havlor said, "We will tell them our offering was accepted, and the *Skaed* has promised to hear our request. What else can we say?"

The two other clerics nodded, a gesture without conviction, void of hope, embracing the necessary lie.

Ingmar clenched his trembling hands in fists. His pulse had only just begun to slow its frantic pace, but every nerve in his body still raced with panic. "They are supposed to protect us," he whispered to Palimo. "How can they hate us so much?"

"Because it's their right," Palimo said. He looked shaken, too, more than Ingmar had ever seen him. "You heard what he said. They owe us nothing. We owe them…we owe them our existence. But why? What's the *point*? All my life I was taught to worship them. I can't worship *that*."

His words barely registered in Ingmar's muddled mind. All he could focus on was Resida, staring vacantly out into the dark emptiness of the temple through colorless eyes, seeing nothing, or infinity. But a sudden movement from Palimo caught his attention, and he turned to see the other boy silently unbutton his green acolyte's robe, revealing the plain white shirt and tan trousers he wore beneath. He let the robe fall in a crumpled heap on the floor and took a step back.

Ingmar watched him aghast. "You're not leaving?"

"I can't stay," Palimo said. "Nor should you. We both saw what we saw. They can't tell us their lies any more—we know the truth. Come with me, brother. Let's tell the world what monsters these Aetherials are."

"What good would that do?" Ingmar asked bitterly. "Better to tell them they don't exist at all."

Palimo shook his head. "How can you stay? After this— how? I thought for sure he would kill you." His gaze darted toward Resida. "Or…or worse."

Ingmar thought a long while, his hands still in knots at his sides. "Because maybe here I can make a difference."

He fell silent as Havlor said to one of the other clerics, "Send word to the palace—quietly. Until we know if *Skaed*

Morayn means to rein in his Guards, we have to do what we can to keep our people safe. Tell the Lord Prince that a nightly curfew is advisable." He paused, then heaved a long sigh. "I don't know what else we can do."

The other cleric bowed in agreement and pushed his way out of the knot of theomancers, past Ingmar and Palimo without a glance at either of them—not even at the rumpled robe lying at Palimo's feet.

Palimo shook his head. "Stay then," he hissed to Ingmar. "I don't care. But I hope you don't expect any rewards or favors from those Aetherial bastards for your faithful service."

"I don't," Ingmar said. "And I wouldn't accept any even if they offered them." He reached out and clasped Palimo's shoulder briefly. "Don't forget me, brother. One day maybe you'll understand why I stayed."

1

NYFALLA — HAUSKELL OF THE SKAED
25 YEARS LATER

UNDER THE STARLIGHT AND THE EMERALD SHINE FROM THE Ankathe's dancing lights, *Skaed* Morayn's face was a flawless riddle. Trelian, High Guard of the *Hauskell*, watched him carefully, sensing instinctively that he stood on perilous ground. He feared the cold contempt in Morayn's silver eyes far more than the hundred foot fall from the fortress's battlements where they stood.

Steeling his nerves, Trelian said, "He deserves to burn."

"Trelian, honestly," said Morayn, leaning his elbows on the merlon. The weariness in his voice cut strangely against the hard light in his eyes; Trelian knew him well enough to recognize the undercurrent of threat simmering beneath those two words. "Emery did nothing wrong."

"You always say that," Trelian said. "But this time one of my brothers lies dead because of him. Reman was a good soldier. He was devoted to you—he would have served you long and faithfully. And now he's *dead*, Morayn. He is lost to Aether, and all because your precious Emery is too reckless to watch his step." He narrowed his eyes and took a step closer to the *Skaed*. On the high battlement, the wind whipped endlessly around them, cold and cutting as hate. "How many more of your guards must die before you rein him in?"

Morayn turned aside, restoring the distance between them. The *Skaed* was finely dressed in rich burgundies and shimmered greys, with a filigreed circlet of silver and rubies ringing his head. It was almost invisible in his hair, but the rubies shone like drops of new blood wherever the light touched it. His fingers, thrumming relentlessly against the wall's glossy black stone, were long and slender, an unnatural bone-white. He wore only a single ring, an obsidian band set with an oblong moonstone on his right thumb. More than the circlet on his head, that ring was the mark of his power. Trelian realized he was staring at its mesmerizing iridescence, as he was always wont to stare, and jerked his gaze away.

"Emery is...complicated," Morayn said, carefully, at length. "If Reman chose to do something stupid and Emery let him do it, why should you blame him for that? Shouldn't you blame Reman for endangering his captain's life? His comrades' lives? If one of them had tried to go back and rescue him...they all might have died. Emery isn't responsible—"

"But he is, damn it!" Trelian ground his teeth and slammed his gloved hand against the wall. "*Skaed*, I mean no disrespect to you at all—"

"And yet you will disrespect my opinion."

Trelian pursed his lips briefly before continuing, "Emery

isn't just complicated. He's *dangerous*. I have never understood why you trusted him with his own guard unit. He goes into the Grey…alone, they say. Without his patrol. Why would anyone do that?" He shifted his weight, fingers clenched tight, then added in a low voice, "There's something…unnatural about him."

"That's my friend you're talking about," Morayn snapped.

"My point exactly. Anyone else would feel the weight of your wrath by now. Him you let do what he wills, damn the consequences. You need to bring him to heel or—"

"Or what?" Morayn demanded, spinning to face him. They stood close now, a bare hand's width apart.

"Take care what you say next, Trelian," said a new voice behind them, and Trelian's eyes widened. It was the only voice he had ever heard that could sound both dangerous and mirthful at the same time. "You're a hair's breadth from treason already."

Trelian dropped a step away from Morayn as the newcomer approached. He was taller than both of them, and there was no silver in his hair or his eyes. Both were black as ink—his eyes so dark they did not even reflect the light of the Ankathe. The long tailored coat he wore was black too, in defiance of Nyfallan fashion, unadorned save the silver star on his shoulder marking his rank. It made him look like a panther, Trelian thought, lithe and lean and dangerous. He saw it even in the way he moved. Aloof, predatory.

Unnatural.

"Emery," he said, with frigid civility.

"We were just talking about you," *Skaed* Morayn said.

14

Trelian gave him a dark glare, but Morayn ignored him as he clasped Emery's arm. Emery eyed them both sidelong.

"What about me?" His lips lifted in an odd smile. "Am I in trouble?"

"If only," Trelian muttered.

Emery took another step closer to him, and Trelian, against all his better intentions, bowed his head and moved back.

"Is there something you want to say to me?"

"I have served in the Nyfallan Guard longer than you have, Emery," Trelian snapped. "I have seniority here. Don't talk down to me like I'm one of your men."

Emery's smile only widened. "Unfortunately for you, I don't talk down to my men. Them I respect."

Trelian bristled. "You killed Reman."

That at least won a look of surprise from Emery. But it faded quickly; he straightened and fixed Trelian with a chilling glare.

"I did not send Reman into the Grey after dawn."

"You told him to watch the theomancers."

"I expected him to use his good sense."

"He was one of your men. You are responsible for what happens to your men." Trelian took a sharp breath, fighting to steady his rising anger. "Perhaps you should think about what example you give to them, *Captain*."

"What I do in my own time is my business," Emery said, turning away. He looked just uncomfortable enough for Trelian to risk a sneer of accusation.

"Did you know Reman was staying overlong in the Grey?" Morayn asked suddenly.

"No. He was with us when we returned to the *Loryan* after our patrol. I only assume something attracted his notice at the last minute, because when we passed through the Mere, he was gone. It was too late to go back by then. The mortals' sun was already rising." He turned to face Trelian again, eyes dark and narrow. "If I had seen him go, I would have gone after him. I would have stopped him."

"Would you?"

"I said it. I don't lie."

"Then answer me this," Trelian said, feeling a thrill of triumph, "and tell me the truth."

"Trelian, no," Morayn said, but Trelian ignored him.

Emery shifted, and waited. Morayn turned away.

Trelian said, "What *are* you?"

The look of bewilderment on Emery's face came and went so quickly, Trelian wasn't sure if he had imagined it; the Captain's expression now was colder than ever. Trelian would have called it haughty, but as he watched Emery with hawkish attention, he saw something like fear in the shadows of his eyes, too deep to hide.

"You have nerve, Trelian," Emery said at length. "What is it you want to know?"

"I want to know where you are from." Trelian took a step forward, relishing the sight of Emery backing away. "You're not like the rest of us."

"What else," Emery said, icily, "could I be like?"

"Trelian, stand down," Morayn interjected, layering the weight of his authority into the words.

"But—"

"I said stand down, or I will relieve you of your commission."

Trelian swallowed hard. Only a fool would risk angering his *Skaed*, and Trelian liked to think he wasn't a fool. For a breathless moment he held his ground, then he inclined his head to Morayn. Before he turned to go, he favored Emery with a bitter smile.

"We aren't finished," he said.

Emery did not return the smile. "Oh," he said. "I think we are."

Arkastel — City of Taris

FAR ACROSS THE MORTAL CITY of Taris, in the high clock tower of the Laysons' district, a bell tolled a single sonorous chime. Even with the dockside tavern windows thrown wide to the cool sea breeze, Therrei tol Dana almost couldn't hear the sound above the raucous laughter and too-loud conversations of half a dozen tipsy patrons. Luckily, she didn't need to hear the sound for herself.

The tavern's hired muscle, a colossus of a man planted just inside the doorway, showing more ink than skin on his bare arms, turned toward the room and bellowed, "One hour till curfew! Bar is now closed."

An odd hush fell over the tavern as the dissatisfied patrons applied themselves to the last of their chosen beverages with professional efficiency. Therrei, sitting beneath one of the open windows with the breeze on her face, twirled her mug of cider indifferently on the grease-stained table. She didn't frequent the tavern for the drink, but because it was the only place she and her closest friend Dessa could both reach before the nightly curfew fell—Therrei coming from the textile mill, Dessa from her bookkeeper's office in the merchants' quarter.

"The clock must be wrong," said a man at the bar, close to Therrei's table.

"Clock's never wrong, fool," his companion said.

"I come to the tavern at exactly the same time and get exactly the same mug of cheap ale every damn evening," the man said, lifting his voice enough that some of the other guests fell silent to listen. "I drink it exactly the same every time. I finish it *exactly* when the bell tolls." He said nothing else, but lifted his mug toward his friend, letting the remaining liquid slosh over the rim.

"You were too busy gabbing tonight, that's all," the other man said. "Drank slower than usual."

"Haven't said a word all night, not that you'd exactly notice. Nights are getting longer, that's what. That's the only explanation."

"Or maybe you're just *exactly* going blind from too much liquor," the bartender jibed, pausing in his relentless effort to polish old beer scum from the stone counter.

A few people muttered in response and Dessa arched her brows skeptically at Therrei, but Therrei couldn't meet her gaze. Other people had been saying the same thing lately. She'd even overheard two of the High Fane's theomancers say it, quietly, under the breath, when they didn't realize she was close enough to hear them.

"The night is getting longer," one had said.

"Will it work?" asked the other.

"He will come. He must come."

Remembering their words, she shuddered. Sometimes she wondered if she heard such things with her physical ears at all—her sense of hearing always felt unnaturally strong. It wouldn't have been the only oddity in her life. Twenty-one years was far too young for her to have heard and seen—and felt—all that she had.

The first man was undeterred. "It's too early. Too soon for the nights to be getting longer."

"Honestly," said the second man, "are you that superstitious? Don't tell me you actually believe those old men and their outdated rituals. Long or short, night is just night. It don't mean a thing at all."

The other patrons nodded in approval, as if by sheer force of will they could transmute his words into truth. Therrei couldn't miss the uneasy undercurrent in the crowd's mood. One of the men, a weathered dockworker of ambiguous age, caught Therrei's eye and grinned.

"You're scaring the women, Traven."

The man at the bar shifted a glance over his shoulder. "They should be scared. Shadow come for them first, I warrant. Easy prey."

Therrei's fingers, needing something to do to keep from trembling, tugged fretfully through her curly mass of auburn hair.

"*Enough*," the bartender said.

Therrei swallowed the last of her cider and slid the mug to the center of the table. "Come on, Dessa," she murmured. "I'm heading home."

But Dessa wasn't listening to her. She planted her hands on the table, sending a frigid glare at the men, and Therrei sighed. She loved her friend dearly, but sometimes Dessa was too brash for her own good. Though she was no prettier than most girls, her spirit was like a candle and she wore her confidence like unbreakable armor. It made people listen to her, whether they wanted to or not. A corner of Therrei's heart had always envied Dessa that ability, even though she preferred to be unnoticed, invisible to most people's idle glances, left alone and quiet. It was easier to ignore people when they ignored you first, and ignoring them was the only way to avoid the pain.

Her fingers curled over her palms.

Dessa didn't know about the pain, though she seemed to have an instinctive understanding of Therrei's wish for isolation. But she had her hackles up now. Therrei could feel the other patrons' attention shifting their way, and while she shrank from it, Dessa met it like a lover's welcome embrace.

"I heard Shadow comes for cowards first," she said, jerking her chin at Traven.

The bartender chuckled, but Traven's face reddened. "You're a fool, girl, talking so flippantly about Shadow."

"Do you have any proof of this Shadow?" Dessa persisted.

Therrei thrummed her fingers against her chin and looked out the window. Every part of her wanted to laugh off the man's fear like Dessa, but deep inside she knew he was right. It wasn't just the hushed conversation of the theomancers that made her believe it. The night *was* getting longer, before its time. Would it continue? Would the darkness grow and grow, until it completely dominated the day? What then? Then… then cold would follow. Cold—and in its wake, famine, and death. What did it mean?

Of course, if Dessa heard her thinking such things, she would laugh. *Why do you listen to those old fools, Rei?* she'd say. *You know they only whisper smoke and riddles to keep people kneeling at their altars. There's no such thing as Aether.*

Over half the people in the city likely shared her opinion, but somehow no one was confident enough in their disbelief to protest the curfews that kept them inside after dark.

Traven shoved his stool away from the bar, drawing Therrei's attention back to the conversation.

"My cousin," he said. Lumbering over, he planted his hands on their table and bent to glare at Dessa. "He was out after curfew, on his farm, trying to get in his stock before the rains. Shadow found him. Struck him down. Left him blathering nonsense, unable to walk, unable to even feed his own damn self. It *ate his soul*, girl. He's no better than a beast now. Just stares off into nothing, day and night, through them creepy colorless eyes."

Dessa, to her credit, didn't flinch back. She was a skeptic through and through; Traven's words wouldn't even faze her. But Therrei shivered and prayed with all her fervor that Traven would go away, because standing this close to her, his fear was seeping into her heart like a slow flood. Fear, grief, horror, outrage. It bled into her palms from the wood of the table, but hard as she tried to pull her hands away, she couldn't. She couldn't do anything.

"Rei?" Dessa asked suddenly.

Traven jerked his head to stare at her too, which only made the feeling ten times stronger.

"You're white as foam." Dessa reached over to clasp her hand. "Gods, your hands are burning up. What's wrong?"

At Dessa's words a few other patrons turned their heads to look at Therrei; she could feel their curiosity like knife points.

Don't look at me, don't look at me...

"Nothing," she whispered. "I'm fine. But...I'm going home. Stay if you like."

Without waiting for Dessa's protest, she scrambled to her feet, tearing her hands away from the table as she did. Grabbing her work bag, she forced herself to walk calmly out of the tavern—even though every instinct was prodding her to run. Run from the pain, run from the unyielding weight of too many staring eyes.

An image of her best friend soul-devoured by Shadow flitted through her mind, and she prayed—foolishly, fervently—that Dessa would have the sense to leave the tavern in time to get home before full night fell.

The remnant shards of Traven's fear and grief slowly faded from her heart as she headed down the street, until all she could feel was a faint lingering unease. Drawing a steadying breath, she turned her steps to the decaying tenement house she called home, as the sun sank too early toward the horizon.

EPISODE 1: GIFTS

PYRIA — PALACE OF THE SUN

THE GOLDEN HOURS OF EVENING cast spears of burnished light into the Sun Palace's white marble hallways, staining the mosaic floors like faded ichor. Atan, Splendor of Pyria, Prince of Light, Glory of the Star, stood in the center of a pool of radiance and stared at the bird staring back at him. One of them, he thought, was in a cage. He hadn't decided which.

The bird was ambivalent to its surroundings, in any event. Walled in by a mesh of copper and gold, the creature seemed content to sit on its cut-branch perch and smooth its brilliant sapphire feathers, content with everything except—possibly—Atan himself standing less than two feet away.

Finished with its preening, the bird shifted its weight to one foot and cocked an eye at Atan. A faint noise behind Atan startled them both. The bird's feathers, faintly ruffled from its preening, abruptly flattened close to its body in alarm. Keeping half his attention on the noise behind him, Atan watched the bird's behavior curiously. It was such a simple creature, and yet, so perfect.

Or perhaps Atan was simply more bored than he had realized.

The sound came closer—footsteps. Just the right amount of noise, so he knew it had to be Jadin. It had taken ages for him to teach his servants not to creep around him, or to bluster through the halls like a windstorm. His personal attendant

Jadin had been the quickest to comply, possibly out of self-preservation. His predecessor hadn't lasted long in the role.

"What do you want, Jadin?" Atan asked. The bird bobbed its head at the sound of his voice, taking a few ungainly steps toward the bars of its cage. There was not room enough for it to fly. "Can't you see how busy I am?"

Jadin cleared his throat softly. "You expressed a desire to attend the Games, Splendor," he said. "The day is almost done, and only the evening Games remain. Shall I send for your litter? Or have you changed your mind?"

Atan mentally filled in the word Jadin hadn't said—*again*.

He had forgotten that he'd told Jadin anything of the sort. The Games were held every week, though Atan rarely went. What did it matter to Jadin if he went this week or the next? It was all such an ordeal—he often felt he was more of a spectacle to the patrons than the performers and athletes and other oddities who filled out the day's festivities. If only he could disguise his identity, he was sure he would enjoy the experience so much more.

Possibly.

He sighed, rubbing his fingertips over the sun-tear on his forehead. The mark was impossible to conceal. All Pyrions had one, though most commoners bore only a single luminous dot—on their forehead or the cheek. Elevation to the nobility merited a second dot on the brow. Atan's was more elaborate than anyone's—save the Star of Pyria's, whose sun-tear was a lacework that framed his eyes and jaw line, touching nose and chin. Compared to that, Atan's was a picture of simplicity. Three arcing lines on his brow, with a single dot beneath. Still, everyone in Pyria recognized that mark...not to mention the inner light that glimmered perpetually beneath the surface of his dark skin.

Jadin was hovering, waiting for his reply, and Atan turned finally to favor him with a glare. The man was half a foot shorter than him, his thick-curling black hair cut in a tonsure. With his head bowed, a scrap of sunlight shone off his bald spot like candlelight on a copper paten.

"I said that?"

"Yes, Splendor."

Atan heaved another dramatic sigh. "Do I have a choice?"

"Of...of course, Splendor," Jadin stammered, bewildered, but Atan just waved him off.

"Very well. Do whatever you have to do to make me presentable."

"Splendor, you are, of course, always presentable exactly as you are..."

Atan threw him a vaguely irritated gesture. "I was tormenting you, Jadin."

The servant, looking flustered, hesitated briefly before shaking his head and beckoning Atan to follow him. Atan glanced one last time at the colorful bird in its gilded cage, then trailed Jadin back into his apartments.

A little less than an hour later, when the evening light was its richest gold, Atan's retinue delivered his litter to the Nexus—the cluster of arenas, tracks, tents and pools where Pyria's most talented or ambitious athletes competed for a chance at honors or titles...or an increase in light. Atan's armed guard, led by their stoic captain, Stelyos, immediately swarmed him as he climbed free of his litter. Jadin stayed close to his side, draped and hooded in deep blue. Of all the Pyrions in attendance, Atan alone wore robes worked in copper and golden silk. Even without the throng of Guards hemming him in, there would be no mistaking him.

"This is a terrible idea. Why did you make me come?" he said to Jadin.

"I—"

Atan waved him off. "Of course you didn't. I know." He glared at the servant. "Obviously."

Gritting his teeth, he made his best show of arrogant indifference as he stalked toward the Grand Arena, where the final event of the day would be held. A gladiatorial contest, Jadin had informed him on the way. The prize for victory was an increase in light and a one-year elevation to the privilege of the nobility. The light itself was taken from the defeated fighter, leaving them a shell, an undesirable, shunned by society until chance or fortune or the long passage of time granted them healing.

"Splendor!"

Atan glanced sharply over his shoulder, only to find Stelyos hurrying to catch up to him, the translucent copper-glass of his halberd flashing in the firelight of the massive braziers that cluttered the plaza. He frowned and paused; he hadn't realized he'd outpaced his retinue—or that he'd begun wandering off in the wrong direction.

"This way, Splendor," Stelyos said, gesturing toward a guarded marble staircase leading to the nobles' boxes.

"I don't want to go that way."

"You cannot—"

"Presuming to give me orders, Stelyos?" Atan asked.

"I think we should allow the Splendor to go wherever he likes," said Jadin, stepping up beside Stelyos and giving the Captain a hard glare. "It is not for us to tell him what to do."

"There, see? I've been given permission by my valet to go where I like."

Jadin's eyes widened. "You of course do not need—"

"Oh, you are all such a dreadful bore," Atan griped, waving them both off, feeling irritable. A few Pyrions stood near the stairwell, watching his entourage with open awe. He didn't want to be seen at all, but the *last* thing he wanted was to be seen arguing with his captain of the guard and his valet. "I am going over there. You may go up to my box if you like."

Jadin bowed and took a step back, but Stelyos stiffened. Though his face remained perfectly neutral, his inner light sparked enough to betray his emotions. Atan just couldn't figure out what they were. Frustration? Anger? Fear? Perhaps all three. Atan caught his eye and gave him a wide smile, which only made the Captain's light flare higher.

Without waiting for Stelyos to issue any dire warnings, Atan turned his steps toward the common section of the amphitheater, where there were no boxes, only rows of stone benches rising above a wide swath of ground edging the arena pit where viewers could stand and watch the event.

"If you are wishing for a good view of the match, Splendor," said Jadin from somewhere behind him, "this is not a good spot. I recommend the next gate."

Atan said nothing. Tamping down his perverse inclination to go exactly where Jadin told him *not* to go, he made his way toward the gate Jadin had indicated. All around him, the crowd of Pyrions making their way into the stands fell back to give him room. With no competition for the best vantage point, Atan climbed to the highest bench and sat at the exact middle of it, and, with arms folded, glared down at the sandy arena floor below. Slowly the other Pyrions filtered into the stands, but with Stelyos's guards posted ominously at the ends of the three highest rows, no one came very close to Atan. That, however, did not keep them from staring.

Jadin, standing behind his left shoulder, suddenly murmured, "Incredible."

"I know," Atan grumbled. "They seem to have forgotten which way to look."

There was a sharp silence, then Jadin said, "Ah, of course, Splendor. But that's not…"

"What then?"

"It was nothing. Just—that Pyrion in the blue robe. Beautiful."

"Jadin," said Atan, rubbing his forehead. "Nine out of ten people in front of me are wearing blue robes. Can you be more specific?"

Jadin shifted his weight, then jerked his chin toward his right. "There, in the row closest to us, near the end."

Atan let his gaze sift over the throng. Most of the Pyrions had finally turned around to watch the two contestants flirting with death in the sands below. But one, a woman with half of her knotted black hair piled on the crown of her head, glanced over her shoulder at that moment to look at him. Jadin was right, Atan decided. There was something striking about her—her eyes, maybe, or perhaps the way she dared to meet his. Before he could figure out what intrigued him, she jerked her gaze away and turned back around.

"Did you see her?" Jadin murmured. "Rare beauty."

Atan made an inarticulate noise, frowning down at the contestants. They'd resorted to wrestling with bare and dusty hands; both had lost their swords, and by the rules of the game, could not pick them up again.

"I suppose I wouldn't mind knowing more about her," he said, absently, at length.

The contestant in the copper-colored tunic suddenly stumbled, and the crowd gasped in horror as a stream of ichor blossomed between his fingers and spilled onto the sand, glimmering like liquid gold.

A horn blared from somewhere down near the pit, and immediately a score of guards rushed from the tunnels to surround the remaining blue-clad fighter.

"What just happened?" asked Atan. Though he knew some of the rules of the contest, this he did not understand.

"He had a knife hidden," Stelyos said. "He stabbed his opponent. By the rules of combat they had both forsaken weapons for hand-fighting."

Atan watched a sudden commotion in the nobles' section of the stands, in the central box where the herald and the Master of the Games sat. They were conferring together, animated, gesticulating frantically at the arena pit. One of their attendant guards suddenly pointed straight at Atan, and the two officials stopped arguing to look in his direction.

"Oh, God," Atan muttered. "They aren't going to make me—"

"Splendor!" the herald cried, raising his arms toward the benches where Atan sat.

"Damn." Atan turned to glare at Stelyos. "How'd he know I was here?"

Stelyos didn't honor the question with an answer. A murmur chased through the gathered crowd and Atan watched the general tide of heads turning his direction— apparently some of the spectators *hadn't* realized that their Splendor was in attendance, and not in his designated box. Atan sighed and got to his feet, and with Stelyos and three other guards on his heels, he made his way down to the stone banister at the bottom of the stands.

"Please, Splendor! Honor us with your wisdom and justice, and adjudicate," the herald called from his station among the nobility's boxes. "What are we to do with this traitor?"

"Traitor?" Atan murmured. He stared down at the offending combatant, who now knelt with his hands clasped above his head in a supplicant's pose. All too aware of Stelyos's hawklike attention, Atan placed his hands on the banister and said to the man, "What do you have to say for yourself?"

He did not raise his voice, but with the dead silence of the crowd, he was certain everyone could hear his words.

The fighter bowed a little lower. "I was desperate, Splendor. I don't know why I did it. I was afraid…I was afraid to lose. I didn't even remember I had the knife on me until it was in my hand."

"Was he going to win?" asked Atan, nodding at the combatant who was lying face-down, unmoving, in the sand.

The other man lowered his arms and raised his head. In his surprise, he dared, for one moment, to meet Atan's gaze.

"I—I don't know."

Atan stared back at him until the man broke and bowed again over his knees. Some muffled word emerged from his crumpled figure.

"Say it so we can hear it!" Atan shouted, letting his voice thunder through the arena.

He could sense more than see the people around him drawing back, cowed by his anger. The supplicant flinched visibly.

"Yes!" he cried. "He was going to win."

"Splendor," Stelyos hissed. "You must not—"

"Must not what, Stelyos? How do you know what I mean to do?"

Stelyos shifted his weight and said nothing.

Atan said, softly, "Am I forgiving?"

A silence, then Stelyos answered, "I don't know, Splendor."

Atan sighed. It would be the easiest thing in the world to draw the Makhdem, the Splendor's Blade of Judgment, and sever the offending combatant from the Aether forever—a traitor's punishment. It would be equally simple to command the guards standing in a ring around him to cut off his hands and his head, an execution that would at least let the Pyrion's spirit return to the Aether.

"*Damn* it all," he muttered.

Without giving Stelyos the slightest opportunity to

intervene, he vaulted over the banister and into the midst of the standing crowd below. They scattered like petals around him as he landed, whispering and horrified and magnetized by his presence—closer to him than any of them had ever come. He heard Stelyos jumping down behind him as he moved forward, but his Captain was a pace behind him as he stepped over the rope perimeter of the arena pit and onto the golden sands.

The guards drew back from their prisoner as he approached; the man was lying prostrate now, in almost the exact pose as his fallen opponent.

"He still has the knife!" one of the guards shouted, and darted forward to snatch it free of the man's hand.

"No need to trouble yourself," said Atan, giving the guard a disarming smile. "He couldn't do anything to hurt me."

The guard looked abashed, but he only saluted and retreated to the line. Atan stopped between the two combatants. A perfect silence shrouded the crowd, as they waited to see what their Splendor would do.

"Splendor, please," Stelyos said, barely a breath.

"Mercy," wept the supplicant.

Ignoring Stelyos, Atan lowered himself to a crouch before the fighter and murmured, "I won't kill you, but you must atone."

He stretched out his hands, letting them hover inches above each of the men's heads. Closing his eyes, he reached deep into the Aether with his *ankamis*, using that innate power to weave his spirit into its eternal essence. He could hear the excited murmur of the crowd but didn't stop, and didn't open his eyes. When the hands of his spirit rested on the spirits of the two men, he who needed no air to breathe, breathed out, and became himself a conduit of the Light.

A sudden motion in the physical world jerked him away from the Aether, and he fell, disoriented, back into his body.

Stelyos was holding him up. Once he had blinked away the Aether's prismatic fog clinging to his vision, Atan saw what he had accomplished. The offending fighter lay shuddering before him, a colorless shell; alive; outcast—the fate he should have faced, if he'd lost the contest fairly. The other combatant, shimmering with a faint light, tried dizzily to pick himself up off the sands. His hand grazed over his chest as he did, feeling the torn fabric, the healed skin beneath. Raising his head, seeing Atan in front of him, he promptly passed out.

Atan grimaced and looked down at his arms. His dark skin was ablaze with light; he was shocked the guards had not turned their faces away.

"Stelyos," he said, his voice unsteady. "Get me out of here. I should never have let you make me come."

"I—" Stelyos started, and sighed. "Yes, Splendor."

2

EMERY WATCHED TRELIAN'S RETREATING FIGURE UNTIL HE HAD disappeared into the Guard Tower at the end of the battlement. With Morayn still standing beside him, watching him keenly, he didn't dare show the turmoil of his thoughts. But they had known each other for as long as Emery had existed, and he knew Morayn was not fooled by his silence.

"Get some rest," the *Skaed* said. "I've put your patrol on temporary leave until you can find a replacement for Reman."

"One less guard—" Emery began, but Morayn held up a hand to silence him.

"Your men lost a brother," he said, sternly. "You lost one of your subordinates. When was the last time that Nyfalla farewelled one of her sons? Let your men have time to process that. You need time. And I don't care what you believe about that."

Emery bent his head and leaned his forearms on the merlon. "You're not wrong," he murmured. After a few moments of heavy silence, he slanted a sidelong glance at

Morayn. "Did you know Trelian was going to ask me that?"

"Yes. At least, I knew he wanted to. I was more surprised that he had the temerity to actually do it."

Emery waved a hand in agreement. "Has he spoken to you about it before?" He paused. "His...doubts that I'm actually Nyfallan?"

"Let it go," Morayn said, a little too quickly. "Trelian is jealous and petty. He's not worth your worry."

"Why would he even ask such a thing?"

"Emery—"

"What else could I possibly be?"

"I *said* let it go."

Emery looked up, surprised by the tightness in his voice, but Morayn refused to meet his gaze. The *Skaed*'s long fingers prodded relentlessly at the black stone of the wall, as if he could find a weakness in its flawless finish.

"Do you realize what a burden you are sometimes?" Morayn asked abruptly. "I don't know what's gotten into you lately. If you only knew how many excuses I've had to give for your stubborn insubordination. How many times I've had to explain away your...inexplicable decisions. You make no sense to me, yet I find myself constantly trying to persuade everyone else that you're sensible. I'm tired of it, Emery. I don't know why I put up with you."

Emery snorted. Morayn's honesty didn't disturb him; Nyfallans were brutally honest to a fault. It would have disturbed him more if Morayn had tempered the barb of his words with honeyed niceties. But they still stung.

"If you weren't my friend, I'd say that's your problem,"

he said. He turned to lean back against the battlement, folding his arms tight over his chest. "Since you are my friend, I'm sorry it's your problem."

Morayn laughed aloud at that, then sobered with a faint shake of his head. "You're an arrogant ass, you know that?"

"Of course. But only sometimes."

"Your definition of *sometimes* does not match mine."

Emery grinned, and Morayn rolled his eyes. For a few moments they stood side by side in the cutting wind, watching the Ankathe dance overhead, its lights now tinged with a faint blood-red hue.

"I do regret what happened to Reman," Emery said softly. "I meant what I said. I—"

"I know." Morayn tipped his head to glance up at him. "You have a dangerous duty. Everyone who joins the Nyfallan Guard knows that, including Trelian. He was a little too eager to be reassigned to fortress watch, after all. I think he has always been afraid of the Grey. And since you seem to have become inordinately fond of the mortals, that makes him afraid of *you.*"

Emery made a noise of disgust, and Morayn held up a hand.

"It's not the mortals or their petty little world he fears," the *Skaed* said, "or that *we* fear—all of us—more than anything. It's that twice-damned sun of theirs. You're reckless enough for twenty men, but even you wouldn't risk facing it. Well—" He paused, then, with a sour look he added, "Again."

Emery pushed away from the wall and would have left without a word, but Morayn suddenly grabbed his arm.

"We belong to Shadow, Emery," he murmured. "I shouldn't have to remind you of that."

Emery studied him through a puzzled frown, then he shook his head and pulled his arm free, and stalked away.

HE MADE HIS WAY DOWN the long stairs of the Guard Tower, carefully avoiding the places he knew the other guards liked to congregate. He didn't stop when he reached the dining hall on the ground floor, but headed straight for the barred wooden door that led far underground. No one noticed him passing by; sometimes Emery imagined he was as unnoticeable in the shadows of Nyfalla as he was in the mortal realm, when he wanted to be—and he relied on that ability more than he cared to admit. It spared him the trouble of dealing with incompetent and irritating people.

Deep underground lay the halls of the fallen. Like the rest of the fortress, the walls were of a cut black stone that shone like rippling cobalt where the light of the pale blue wisp lanterns touched. The ceiling was so high it was lost in the shadows, but the corridors were narrow enough to feel claustrophobic. Set in deep niches along each wall were stones etched in naming runes, shining with a mercurial glimmer in the low light. Behind most of the marker stones were the bodies of Nyfallans who had been killed in the last great war of the Aethers.

One was newly cut, and the niche behind it was empty.

Emery laid his hand against the rune carvings, regret weighing heavy on his mind. Reman had been a good soldier, too good to see his life cut short in such a meaningless way. Like the Pyrions of Light, Nyfallans were immortal so long as they stayed in their element. By violence, by the stroke of justice, or even by the proximity of their opposite element they could be killed or injured—but otherwise, death was something each Aetherial chose freely when they reached what they felt was the end of their time. It wasn't even a death the way mortals died. They simply returned to their Aether.

And now Shadow had called home one of its own, before his time.

"Why did you go back?" Emery murmured to the empty burial niche. "What did you see?"

He bent his head, eyes closed. Another question gnawed at the back of his mind, compounding his regret.

"Why didn't I?"

He didn't realize he'd spoken out loud until someone behind him said, "Why didn't you what?"

Emery spun, only to find one of his fellow captains leaning on the opposite wall. They had served together since Emery had first joined the Guard, and though Emery called few people *friend*, he counted Brana among that number.

He sighed and let his fingers drift over the cold runes again. "Reman must have seen something in the Grey, and gone back to investigate. I can't help wondering…why didn't I see it? I should have been the one to notice it. I should have been the one to go back."

Brana gave an undignified snort. "Maybe he forgot his knife."

"I wish it had been that simple," Emery said, smiling faintly.

"Why couldn't it have been? Nothing interesting happens in the Grey. Nothing they do affects us. Most of them don't even believe we exist...or they believe we're some kind of monster that's behind every bad thing that happens to them."

Emery didn't answer. In the silence that followed, Brana studied him through a faint frown, staring at him so long that Emery felt uneasy. Whatever it was that made Trelian doubt him—did Brana see it too?

"You almost sound like you *want* there to be something wrong," Brana added.

"That's absurd," Emery muttered.

"Do you just want an excuse to wander around the Grey? Everyone knows you spend too much time there. It isn't *safe*."

Emery took a step toward him. "Safe?" he said, the word traced with laughter. "How is it not safe?"

"We don't belong there, Emery. Being there...it changes us. Weakens us." Brana paused. To his credit, he didn't back away. "It isn't safe."

Emery's lips lifted in a cold smile. "Safe is boring, Brana."

"Safe lets us survive."

"What kind of existence is this?"

Brana's eyes widened. "The kind that fulfills our nature," he said. "Nyfalla is perfection."

"And yet Reman is dead."

"Because he strayed out of Nyfalla when he shouldn't have."

Emery flung his hands up in disgust and turned away. There were no words for the nagging frustration in the back of his mind. No explanation for the shapeless worry that haunted him. Somewhere under the surface of Nyfalla's perfection was a fatal crack, and Emery was determined to bring it to light. But first he had to find out what it was.

He looked one last time at Reman's burial niche.

He knew exactly where to begin.

THE FALLING SUN HAD BARELY grazed the ridge of the mountains when Therrei arrived, breathless and chilled, at the door of her tenement house. Biting her lip in focus, she eased the heavy door open and slipped, quietly as she could, into the dank darkness of the foyer.

"Therrei, that you?" a shrill voice called, wavering out from the shadows.

Therrei sighed and let the door settle shut behind her. "Yes, Sera."

"Speak up, girl! Can never hear a word you say! Between you and that good-for-nothing Garm I'd think my ears were sick as a corpse. He creeps about too, and whispers so he thinks I can't hear him. Up to no good, the pair of you."

Being connected in any way to the repulsive Garm made Therrei's blood boil, but she didn't rise to the bait. As her vision adjusted to the dim light, she eyed the crumpled woman perched on the hallway bench. The landlady always reminded Therrei of an old raven, bitter and gnarled, shrouded in a mass of unkempt feathers. Only the tip of her lumpy nose protruded past the cap she wore, dingy lace and velvet that never seemed to fit her. The way she sat, tipped forward with her weight braced against a knotted cane, made her look like she was about to dive on some unsuspecting bit of carrion.

Therrei took a slow, quiet breath and moved toward the stairwell. Her boots made hardly any sound as she slipped through the hall, but Sera, for all her complaints, had ears like a hawk. Therrei had almost succeeded in creeping past her when the old woman's hand lashed out and fixed on her forearm.

"Didn't hear you come in last night."

Therrei shot a glance at Sera's face, wrinkled and compressed like a dried grape, her clouded, red-rimmed eyes fixed somewhere to Therrei's left. She wondered if the woman stayed up at night counting as each of her tenants came home. Strange old crone.

Therrei tugged her arm free. "I did come in," she muttered. "Do you think I don't have sense to stay out of the night?"

"Testy," Sera said, waving her hand to try to find Therrei's arm again. "Where's that friend of yours? Suppose he'll be coming back some time soon. You know what I say to that, Therrei. I won't have that nonsense in my building."

Therrei froze, suddenly cold all over. "Friend? What friend?" she asked. "No friend of mine has ever come here."

I'd be too ashamed, she thought, but didn't have the heart to say it out loud.

"Strange sounding man," Sera said, nodding sagely. "All proper and polite, out of his element down quayside, I thought.

Said he needed a word with you. *Said* it was important. Lies, I'm sure."

An uneasy chill crept down Therrei's arms. "When... when was this person here?"

Sera kept batting the air, until finally Therrei relented and held out her arm for the woman to grab.

"Oh, three, maybe four days ago."

"*Three days!*" Therrei cried. "But I saw you yesterday morning! Why didn't you tell..."

Sera shrugged dismissively, her black knitted shawl slipping off her bony shoulders. Even tangled in a knot of fear and frustration, Therrei couldn't resist reaching out to fix it.

"Suppose I didn't think of it," Sera said, clutching the moth-eaten wool close to her throat. "Like I said—lies, the lot of it. You know how those men are. Saying anything they can think of to slip past old Sera." She tapped the side of her nose meaningfully.

"I wouldn't know about that," Therrei said, blushing. "Sera, please. I need to go to sleep. It's already later than I meant to get back."

"Yes, yes. But tomorrow is Ganrashin. You don't have to work, do you?"

"No, but that doesn't mean I'm not tired. I worked all day *today.*"

"Hmph," Sera snorted. "I can tell. You stink like dye and wool. At least I caught you this time. Had me up worrying half the night, thinking Shadow'd got you."

Sera released her arm, and Therrei took a few tentative steps away. The old woman had actually been worried about her? The idea that Sera—or anyone—would fret over her moved Therrei strangely. And then, though she didn't know why, she went back and took Sera's gnarled hand.

"Thank you," she murmured. "I'm sorry. I didn't mean to make you anxious."

Sera gave a wheezing laugh. "I ain't sentimental, girl. If you'd got eaten by Shadow, who'd pay your rent? D'you know how hard it is to get tenants these days?"

Therrei stared at her a moment, then, sighing, she shook her head and left the old woman to her vigil.

Once in her room she moved by habit, while her thoughts scattered and jumped from one question to another, locust-quick and chaotic. Reluctantly she shed her heavy wool coat, then sat on the edge of her rickety bed to pull off her boots. She left both pairs of her woolen stockings on, then shoved a bit of coal into her stove to warm the drafty room. As the heat crept through the tiny space, she sat on the wooden stool beside it and buried her face in her hands. Her whole body trembled, and she knew it had nothing to do with the cold.

Who could possibly have tracked her to the tenement house? Even Dessa didn't know where she lived, and she was Therrei's closest and oldest friend. Her employer, Gavin, didn't know. The only way someone could possibly have found out was if they had tailed her from the tavern, or from the workhouse—without her knowledge. The notion sent her thoughts ringing with alarm. She was vigilant to the point that Dessa called it paranoia, always hyper-aware of her surroundings. Who was where around her. What they were doing. Where they were looking.

Surely she would have known if someone had been following her.

Surely she would have felt the weight of their attention.

Shivering, she climbed under the blankets and tried to ignore the old building's ominous creaks and groans long enough to chase down restless sleep, but she couldn't ignore the question chattering in the back of her mind.

She was nobody. She was *deliberately* nobody. So who would possibly know enough about her to care—and to care enough to follow her?

It was with that question tangling her thoughts into chaos that she finally fell asleep.

ATAN'S LITTER DELIVERED HIM TO the steps of the palace just as the last light of day faded past the gold-gilt domes, leaving the sky a wash of tawny copper. Fires burned in countless brass braziers and in lamps hung on every marble wall, replacing what light and warmth the evening had stolen away. Jadin and Stelyos helped Atan from the litter and onto a carried chair, and Atan did not even have the energy to complain about the excessive attention.

A small army of servants immediately swarmed the chair like scarabs. As they hurried to lift him up and carry him toward the palace, Atan caught Stelyos's worried glance. If he had to hazard a guess, he would have said Stelyos was angry—but at what, or whom, he didn't know. Likely he was angry at Atan himself, and Atan grudgingly admitted that he rather deserved it. He maintained an uncharacteristic silence the entire way into the palace, and when his servants deposited him on his silk-draped couch, he dismissed them all with a wave.

Jadin hovered a moment, perturbed to be sent away with the lower staff, but Atan skewered him with a savage glare that sent him scuttling out on their heels without so much as a backwards glance. Stelyos stood stalwartly at the edge of the lattice screen, both hands braced on the haft of his halberd.

"I thought I dismissed you," Atan said, lying back on his pillows.

"I'm not one of your servants," Stelyos said.

Atan snorted and reached toward the goblet one of his attendants had left on the table near his head, but his arm shook so violently that he doubted he could even lift the cup. Letting let his hand drop back on the couch, he turned to stare out the window at the sultry night.

Stelyos, watching impassive from his post, said after a moment, "Can I get you your wine?"

"I don't want it."

Deferring to his wishes, Stelyos made no response, and didn't move. Atan felt oddly relieved that Stelyos hadn't leapt forward to retrieve the goblet for him; he expected that fawning subservience from Jadin, but Stelyos was disciplined to the point of rigidity.

"Why don't you go away?" Atan said. "I'm not going

anywhere, and I'm not in any danger."

"That judgment is my prerogative, Splendor," Stelyos replied.

Atan grumbled and turned a little further on his side. He didn't want to sleep, though he desperately needed it. In sleep he would wander the outermost rim of his Aether, drawing its life and energy back into his soul, restoring him to his natural strength...but something deep inside him shied away from the thought of drawing so near to the Aether again. He had come closer to it that evening than he had in a long time, and the memory of it still sang in his veins, luring him back again with a strange magnetism.

It was said that the Aether was always calling out to her children in sleep, drawing them back to her embrace. Every Aetherial would face the night when the song was too sweet to resist, and then they would wake no more. For most of his life Atan had successfully avoided thinking about that, but in moments like this, when he had gone too far in using his *ankamis,* he felt the draw of the Aether so deeply it terrified him to the roots of his soul.

"I'm tired," he complained to the wall. "Why can't I get rest without sleeping? It isn't fair."

Stelyos said nothing.

"Have you ever...have you ever been afraid of falling asleep?"

The silence carried on, until finally Atan, too curious for his own good, glanced at Stelyos over his shoulder. The guard was watching him through a faint frown, apparently uncertain if Atan actually wanted him to answer.

At length he shifted his weight and said, "Only once, but it was before I was assigned to your personal guard, Splendor. I was serving in the Pyrion Guard then."

He left it at that, which piqued Atan's curiosity to an unbearable level. "And?" he asked, rolling onto his back to see Stelyos better. "What happened?"

"I was caught in shadows, in the Grey," Stelyos said. He looked pained by the memory, or vexed by Atan's attention; he kept his gaze riveted on the pole of his halberd. "I was badly weakened. All I wanted was to sleep." He glanced up at Atan briefly, then at the halberd again. "I was out in the open, and it was nearing evening. The rest of my unit had scattered. If I had fallen asleep, either the dark of night would have claimed me, or Aether would have."

"Are you still shadow-torn?" Atan asked. It was a deeply personal question, but Atan had no qualms about making Stelyos uncomfortable.

"I am, Splendor," Stelyos answered after a moment. "But it was only on my back."

Atan eyed him sidelong. "Does it still hurt?"

"Not any more."

Tucking his hands behind his head, Atan sighed and stared up at the skylights, at the copper nightfall. "Sometimes I wonder if I was in the Pyrion Guard, once. Before the Star made me his heir."

There was a curious silence, then Stelyos ventured, "Do you not remember?"

"I only recall a very few things from that life."

Atan could feel the burn of Stelyos's curiosity, and stifled a smile. He had every right to know his guard's secrets, but Stelyos had no such right to hear his. Still, he wondered idly what Stelyos would say, if he knew what Atan remembered.

"Why do you think you might have been a Guard?" A pause, then Stelyos added, almost a whisper, "Do *you* have a shadow-wound?"

"God, no," Atan said. "But I feel like I know the Grey. Like I've been there before. And more than anything…I wish that I could go back."

It was a woman's face.

Of all the fragmented memories he held from that life before, hoarded carefully away like the sun dragon's tears, this one alone felt certain. But he remembered nothing else about her. Only her eyes—mercurial grey. Full of fear. Full of hope.

He sighed again and rubbed a hand over his face. It was so long ago now, he wondered if she were even still alive. Mortals' lives were so very short.

"I'm going to sleep now, Stelyos," he said. "If you see me fading into Aether, wake me up, won't you?"

FROM HIS PLACE JUST ABOVE THE SLATE ROOFTOP OF A WEATHERED hostel, deep in the heart of the Grey, Emery watched the mortals' sun rise.

Their world spread below his feet in the colorless wash of his Darksight—the sea troubled as ink, shadowed and vast; Taris's cobbled streets weaving ant trails between the narrow stone buildings; the light flickering and blurred behind the frosted glass panes of the street lamps, like fool's fire in fog. Even the smoke curling from the forest of chimney stacks was little more than a pale hint in the murk, and eastward over the docks and quay, a dim swirl of clouds moped just above the ocean horizon, veiling the rising sun like an eyelid.

If he stepped inside the Grey, the world would burst into color around him. The eastern sky might be a sultry copper or a shy peach, or a riot of ardent reds, ushering in the new day with glorious pageantry. But there in the *Loryan*, the liminal space between the worlds, it all looked grey. It was why the Aetherials of both Pyria and Nyfalla gave that mocking name to the mortals' realm. Emery longed to see the colors again.

But this time no one was there to pull him back from the sun, and Emery wasn't ready to die.

He pressed his hands a little harder against the boundary veil between the worlds. All he could think of was Reman, trapped in the Grey after dawn. When Emery and his patrol had returned that night, there hadn't been enough left of their comrade to bear back to Nyfalla for burial. Trelian's words echoed, sharp and accusing, in Emery's mind. Was he responsible for Reman's death? Emery had been his captain. He should have noticed Reman turning back.

He should have saved him.

Guilt and grief burned in his soul, and he closed his eyes briefly to silence them.

I couldn't have saved him, he thought. *It was too late the moment he incarnated.*

But maybe I…

He silenced that thought too. With a shudder he edged lower, until he crouched so close to the rooftop he could almost imagine he was touching it. In the street below, a lamper made his rounds, extinguishing the street lamps one by one as the night faded to sunrise. Emery could barely see him. Wrapped in a dark coat and hood, the man looked half as much a Shadow as Emery himself.

A distant, muffled sound reached Emery's ears—a clock tower bell, chiming the sunrise. It was still ringing as the streets woke up. Townsfolk trickled out onto their front stoops, most well-wrapped in long coats and hats against the morning chill. On most days he could guess which way they would move down the street based on what they wore—the ones in heavy oilskin coats and thick boots, burdened with lumpy linen sacks, mainly headed south and east toward the docks and boats. The better-dressed ones with the leather satchels would move northwest toward the markets and guild halls, or if they were lucky, the Laysons' parliaments.

Today was what the mortals called Ganrashin, a day of rest, a market-day, a day of idle pleasures and frivolities. Those who had no choice went toward their work on the docks; those who could afford the leisure moved toward the Upper City.

Emery's patrol didn't often venture into those districts of Taris. Amura and her more senior unit preferred that beat, not because it was safer—all the streets of all the towns and cities in Arkastel were generally abandoned at night because of the last Lord Prince's ridiculous curfew—but because, as Amura had once told him, it smelled better. Emery couldn't fault her for that. When Nyfallans incarnated in the mortal world, all their senses were abnormally heightened. Taste and touch were tolerable but smell and sound were nearly overpowering, and any semblance of light was crippling. Sometimes Emery wondered if he was the only Nyfallan who craved the risk and the breathless expectation of terror.

Slowly, other sensations crept into his awareness. The warbling of a lone songbird, a cheerful reverie against the harsh jarring of the gulls that never slept. The faint odor of woodsmoke. A cool, dank wind kissing his cheek.

And beneath his feet, the solidity of a slate roof, sloped, slick from the night's fog. He jerked back from the world, hands

51

clenched reflexively. There in the comforting nothingness of the *Loryan*, he collected himself and refocused his energies. It was now too close to daybreak for him to incarnate. Even in the shadow of the chimney stack, the light was already too strong.

He could almost imagine the pain of burning. It was the only real pain a Shadow could feel.

"Therrei!" someone shouted from the Grey below.

Even from the cloister of the *Loryan* Emery could hear the voice clearly. He moved a little forward in the veil for a clearer view, and lowered himself down as if he were actually sitting on the roof. Across the street a ramshackle tenement house sagged against its neighbor, its salt-weathered wooden beams tilting crazily, its roof warped and crooked. The front door hung open, and a bundled figure stood on the stoop. Emery couldn't see anything more clearly, and he couldn't push the *Loryan* further without running the risk of incarnating unintentionally. The *Loryan* could only bring him so close to the mortal world before it broke, following the contours of the world's geography and cities. The rooftop was almost too close already.

"Therrei, your rent or I'll have Garm throw your things on the street!"

"But I won't get paid until tomorrow!" the figure called back, leaning through the doorway. "I'll pay you then."

From the sound of the voice, Emery guessed she was a woman, young in the way of mortals, barely out of her girlhood. He watched with idle curiosity as she tugged her hood forward, lingering on the front stoop with her gaze riveted on the eastern horizon. But she didn't make her way toward the docks. Emery could only wonder what the sunrise must have looked like, to hold her so captivated.

The wind bit his cheeks and he flinched back again. Cursing himself for his recklessness, he battled back a surge of regret, and longing.

And then, for one brief, bewildering moment, the girl turned and stared straight at him. Emery was so certain she could see him, he had to check himself to make sure he hadn't incarnated accidentally. But no, he was still safe within the *Loryan*...and yet she seemed to see straight into his soul. In another minute she was gone, trudging up the street toward the market district. Emery watched her go, strangely shaken.

"You weren't thinking of looking, were you?"

Emery jumped in spite of himself, half-turning to watch as a Shadow moved toward him through the eerie emptiness of the *Loryan*, silhouetted by the silver-blue lights of the Mere that formed the portal to Nyfalla.

"I might now that you're here, Morayn," he said, smiling faintly at his *Skaed*. "You can carry me back to the Ward if I get burned."

Morayn gave an exaggerated groan as he dropped down beside Emery, tugging his hands through his silver-black hair. "Don't, please. I might just leave you in the street this time and watch you squirm. It would make Trelian happy, anyway."

Emery gave him a savage smile and turned back to the city.

"I couldn't believe it when I found out you were here again," Morayn said. "What did I tell you last night? Your patrol is off duty. You're *supposed* to be taking leave. What exactly do you find so fascinating in the Grey?"

"Nothing that would interest you."

Morayn surveyed the streets below distastefully. "You could at least pick a nicer city to visit. I've heard tell of some nice towns down south, away from the coast. Have you been to Markala? Leros says—"

"Villages," Emery scoffed. "Taris is the capital city. Anything interesting that is going to happen in the Grey will start here."

"That's exactly the problem with you, Emery," Morayn sighed. "Nothing interesting is ever going to happen in the Grey. The Grey doesn't matter. The mortals don't matter. They imagine we care if they live or die, but why should we? Their lives are petty and short and meaningless. Their *world* is petty and meaningless."

"If that were true, we wouldn't patrol its streets. They are part of the balance."

"Fine, so we care about the Wall. But that is all."

Emery slanted him a sidelong glance. "Then why are you here?"

"Looking for you, of all things. Kohla told me to keep you out of trouble. I think she meant for me to keep you away from the Greys, but how am I to stop you? You don't listen to anyone."

Emery grumbled. Kohla was the last person in Nyfalla he wanted to know about his off-duty journeys to the Grey, but somehow she always found out. They said it was her sight—not her eyes, but her spirit. They said she could just focus on someone and know exactly where they'd been... even where they meant to go. Emery wasn't sure if that was true, but the old woman was terrifying enough without the myths of mystic powers. Perhaps that was because she was an old woman. Emery wasn't entirely sure what she was, but she wasn't pure-blooded Nyfallan. Age did not exist within the Aethers.

I wonder if Trelian has asked her what she *is,* he thought bitterly.

After a moment he glanced back at Morayn, speculative. "Kohla Saw me here...but you didn't?"

Morayn returned the look with a dangerous glare. "What I See, and what I do not See, are none of your concern, *Captain.*"

Emery's brows lifted in faint surprise but he looked away, and didn't press the matter. Morayn's *ginnregin* was not something they often discussed, but the *Skaed* had never rebuffed Emery's questions so violently. Emery could sense instinctively that Morayn was troubled, but he knew better than to ask when his friend's spirit was already riled.

He could feel Morayn's attention fixed on him, but for a few moments he stared stubbornly at the worn tips of his boots. They were all black, as plain and unadorned as the rest of his garb. Flamboyance had never been his style, unlike Morayn, who always dressed in gaudy silver and deep jewel reds. Morayn said it was because Emery spent too much time watching the Greys. After his conversation with Trelian last night, Emery wondered if that was the only reason.

"We shouldn't call it the Grey," he said, abruptly.

A pause. "But it is. Look at it."

"Not if you've seen it, Morayn. *Really* seen it. It's only grey here. Only grey to Aetherials too frightened to step out of their realms. But there are so many colors—colors we could never even imagine in Nyfalla. At sunrise it's particularly beautiful. Have you ever seen a blue so bright it hurt your eyes?"

Morayn arched a brow. "Why would I want to? That sounds terrible."

"It is. Terrible…and exhilarating."

"Trelian is right. You are absolutely mad."

"Trelian doesn't think I'm mad," Emery said blandly. "He thinks I'm dangerous."

"Point taken." Morayn smacked him on the shoulder, gesturing back at the Mere where they'd passed into the *Loryan*. "Nyfalla is beautiful, Emery. What you're talking about is…it's just a shadow."

"You do realize how foolish that sounds?" Emery asked.

Morayn didn't answer.

Emery had often wondered what the Greys would think if they could see the night sky of Nyfalla—millions of stars woven between nebulous swirls of red and gold, the Ankathe's green rivers of light tracing in an eternal snakelike dance over the realm, three moons bathing the realm in a dusky glow. The mortals' night sky was a dull wash of silver and black, and only that when clouds didn't obscure the stars. Sometimes, when the Ankathe appeared in the Grey, the mortals could see those dancing ribbons of light—though, fittingly, they merely looked a faint grey to the human eye. The mortals called it an omen. Some called it a curse. It was neither of those things, of course, but that didn't matter. If something appeared in the night sky, the mortals saw it as a precursor of evil things to come. Always.

Good things came during the day.

Evil things came by night.

So why do I care?

But no matter how hard he tried to come up with an explanation that made some kind of sense, he simply couldn't.

"I would see it again if I could," he murmured, dropping his gaze. "The sunrise."

Morayn cursed softly. "You know what they told you would happen."

Emery shrugged, taking a perverse pleasure in how much it annoyed Morayn. The *Skaed* flung his hands into the air with an inarticulate groan.

"And it doesn't even seem to bother you. Next thing you know, you're going to tell me you want to see Pyria."

"Do you think I'm crazy?"

Morayn gave a little shrug of his hands, as if it were obvious.

"Actually, don't answer that."

He stood, lending Morayn a hand to pull him to his feet. Morayn stood squarely in front of him, ignoring the six-inch difference in height that made him cant his head back to meet Emery's gaze.

"I already did. You *are* crazy."

"And you're an idiot."

Morayn grinned. "I could hang you for talking to your *Skaed* that way."

"You could try."

Morayn shook his head and turned to go, Emery following reluctantly behind. But something at the corner of his eye made Emery jerk to a stop, and turn back for one moment to look at the city street below. A flash—copper, maybe, strangely bright in the gloaming.

A sudden flash of heat surged through him, steel-sharp, unrelenting.

He staggered, hands lurching out to grab something, anything, for balance. He must have cried out, because Morayn was beside him in an instant, hands catching his shoulders.

"What in hell-light is wrong with you?"

Emery gripped his arms, body rigid with pain. "You can't feel it? Morayn…go. *Go!* We have to…"

His voice died, and he just waved noiselessly at the sky above. Morayn backed a step away from him, and Emery, cursing profoundly, positioned himself between his *Skaed* and the Grey as he drove Morayn ahead of him. The heat flared, like the tips of white-hot daggers tracing the line of Emery's spine and ribs. His back arched convulsively. Morayn reached back and grabbed his arm, ignoring Emery's futile rebukes as he hauled him stumbling forward.

The Mere hung in the air in front of them. Its ghosting swirls of silver-blue looked almost liquid, rippling and shimmering sporadically with its own light. A metallic resonance rang in Emery's ears, louder and more intense the closer they came. It was the worst part about crossing over—sometimes the noise lingered in his head for hours. But at that moment Emery couldn't imagine a more beautiful sound. Within three steps they had passed through the Mere, and seconds later they emerged on its shores within the safety of Nyfalla. From this side the Mere looked like a glassy pond, reflecting the nebulae and stars above.

Emery fell to his knees in the grass beside it, careful not to touch its surface again. Close by he could see the red velvet of Morayn's shoes. The *Skaed* was crouching beside him, all concern and worry, but Emery refused to look at him. He clenched and unclenched his hands, trying to control their shaking.

"What happened?" Morayn asked.

Emery bowed his head and didn't answer. After a minute Morayn shoved him, hard, and shouted the question again.

"You couldn't feel it?" Emery asked, disbelieving. "Why not?"

"Feel what?"

"The Pyrion." Morayn stared at him, wide-eyed and speechless. "He was incarnating right below us."

"You *saw* him?"

Emery gave him a bland look. "The sun wasn't high enough for him to incarnate unaided. He was carrying a sunbrand, Morayn. That's what I felt. Have you ever felt one of those things? They burn like the damn sun itself, all the way into the *Loryan*. If I'd stayed to get a good look at it, I probably wouldn't be here right now."

"Well, neither of us would be here if it weren't for your... whatever strange power that was." Morayn paused, and narrowed his eyes. "You've felt one before."

Emery nodded, wary.

"That was the last time, wasn't it? When I pulled you back?"

"Yes."

"You didn't die then. And you didn't die this time, either."

"Obviously." Emery avoided his gaze. "What's your point?"

"It's just… Doesn't it worry you?"

"Why should it?" Emery asked, deliberately obtuse.

Morayn glared at him. "I just think, if it had been me, I would not have survived. If you hadn't shielded me…"

It wasn't gratitude, but the unspoken acknowledgment was the best Emery could hope for. Trelian's question echoed endlessly in the back of his mind. He ground his teeth and stared at the Mere, trying, and failing, to ignore it.

What are you?

"Maybe I'm just more attuned to their presence than you are, because I've been in the Guard so long. Maybe I can just sense it before it becomes dangerous. Most of us don't…" He broke off, wincing as the last traces of heat curled through him and faded away. "…don't wander around in the Grey when we might encounter them."

"Yes, Emery, as we've already established, most of us aren't insane."

Emery sat back on his heels, shifting his gaze to the sky for calm. Morayn was right. That would not have been the first Pyrion he had met. The Pyrion guards patrolled the mortal realm during the day, just as the Shadow guards of Nyfalla did during the night, and he realized without the faintest tinge of regret that he had a bad habit of overstaying his welcome in the Grey. The last time he'd crossed paths with a Pyrion at the grey half-light of dusk, he'd been too busy watching the crowds to notice the slow searing heat that presaged the guard's incarnation. They'd kept him in the infirmary for two days after Morayn dragged him back to Nyfalla, because everyone believed he'd been at the doorway of death.

Emery had never told anyone the truth.

"What's wrong with you?" Morayn asked, breaking the thick silence. "You look worried. You never look worried." He paused. "It makes *me* worried."

Emery snorted. "I don't know. Something felt different today."

"Here, or in the Grey? Or do you mean the Pyrion?"

Emery hesitated, trying to sift through his own uncertainties. The nagging worry at the back of his mind was shapeless, spectral; he knew no words that would give it form.

"I was in the *Loryan* because something felt wrong," he said. "I wanted to see if anything odd was happening in the Grey, something that Reman might have noticed." He shrugged. "I didn't see anything unusual, but I've never felt anything like this. Not as long as I've existed."

Morayn shifted his weight uncomfortably. When Emery shot him a curious glance, he looked away.

"What?"

"Stay out of the Grey, Emery," he said. "I don't like what it does to you."

"What does that even mean?" Emery asked, but Morayn, with a mountain's stubbornness, refused to answer. Emery gritted his teeth. "If you let me take you with me some time—"

"*No.*"

Emery startled at the violence of the word.

"I only go into the Grey to rescue you, and then only when Kohla makes me," said Morayn. "Me, your *Skaed*, putting myself in danger to save your pathetic hide. What do you say to that? Blessed Night, what would *Trelian* say to that?"

"Terrifying to think my lord is so impressionable that a frail old woman can force him out of his palace."

He barely saw Morayn draw back his arm, but just in time he ducked aside to avoid the punch. Morayn stood up, fists clenched, doing his best to tower over Emery's half-prostrate figure.

"Say that again?"

Emery laughed quietly and picked himself up, this time not even bothering to hide how much taller he was than his *Skaed*. He gripped Morayn's shoulder, still grinning.

"Whose fault is it we're still alive?"

Morayn shoved his hand off and strode a few paces away. "That was the last time," he said over his shoulder. "I mean it. I'll issue a royal prohibition against venturing into the Grey without orders if I have to. You're a magnet for those fiends and I wouldn't much blame them if they burned you." He turned around, walking a few steps backward, fear or anger in his eyes. "Damn your pride, Emery. Why won't you ever listen to me? You never could listen to anyone but yourself. You'll be the only one to blame if it gets you into trouble, and I'm not always going to be there to save you."

It was possible he kept talking, but he had turned again,

and moved so far away that his voice trailed off into the windless dark.

"Just like last time," Emery said to himself.

UNDER THE DAWN OF BRILLIANT golden light at the heart of the Sun Palace, the tiger sprawled like a house cat on a patch of smooth stone. Atan watched the creature sleeping from an overhanging balcony with an odd feeling of solidarity. If he thought the animal wouldn't tear his head off, he imagined he'd be right down there in the menagerie with it, sleeping in the slant of morning sun. His muscles felt sluggish, and his mind was astonishingly vacant.

He was bored to death.

"Splendor," someone said, stepping out onto the balcony behind him—Jadin, of course. It was always Jadin blustering in when he wasn't needed, or wanted.

Just because I'm bored doesn't mean I want to be bothered, Atan groused to himself.

"What do you want this time?" he asked, leaning his arms on the white marble balustrade. Below, the tiger lifted its head at the sound of his voice, then flopped back onto the stone. "I don't want to go to the Games today. I don't want to go tomorrow. You tricked me into going last night, and now look at me. I've barely recovered. You'll be the death of me, Jadin."

He lifted his arms with a wide flourish of his hands, as if that proved anything. Jadin made an undignified noise that might have been a snort, unsuccessfully concealed in a cough.

"Splendor, you asked me to bring you Leyala."

"Who?"

He turned, finally, to face his servant. Jadin didn't look up when Atan turned, which both pleased and annoyed him.

"The girl, Leyala," Jadin said. "You saw her at the Games yesterday."

Atan racked his memory, trying to recall what girl Jadin was talking about. Whoever she was, Atan had completely forgotten about her. It surprised him that Jadin had remembered, but then, it was Jadin's job to remember.

He stalked past the servant on his way into his chambers. The open skylights in the gold-leafed ceiling let rich mosaics of light dance over the white-tiled floor, and a soft, warm wind rippled the sheer sapphire drapes that divided the chamber into meaningful spaces. In the very center of his apartments stood a marble fountain sculpted in the form of two battling eagles, with palms and ferns and orange trees surrounding it like a desert oasis. Atan often imagined that the constant hushed murmur of trickling water and the tangy citrus smell of the air were the only things saving him from plunging finally and entirely into madness.

He went to sit on the lip of the fountain by habit, trailing Jadin forgotten behind him. When he glanced up and found the servant hovering nearby, still with bowed head, he let out a sharp breath of frustration.

"What do you *want?*"

"Should I bring her to you or not?" Jadin asked,

unperturbed by Atan's outburst.

"No," Atan snapped. "Yes, fine. I don't care. Do what you want. God, what's the point anyway?"

Jadin wisely made no answer, since he certainly didn't qualify as the person to whom the question was addressed. He only offered a low bow and moved away, his sandals tapping on the floor beneath the swirl of his blue robes. Atan watched him go, then waited with idle curiosity for him to return. His fingers trailed in the cool water of the fountain, feeling its tiny current sweep past and tug at the seven heavy gold bands he wore on his left hand.

Absently he plucked one off—a simple ring set with a sapphire—and let it drop to the bottom of the fountain. A small collection of rings congregated there, made myriad by the refracted light, waiting to be gathered up or forgotten. He didn't know why he did it; he was making no offering; the gesture was meaningless. But it was a habit. He had more than enough gaudy jewels to spare, and he was half sick of them all anyway.

A quiet murmur of voices broke the sanctuary of his chambers, then the sound of returning footsteps.

"You'll find him by the fountain, miss," Jadin said. "I'll leave you here."

Atan listened to his retreating steps and waited for the girl to approach, but for some time nothing happened.

Feeling irritable, he said, loudly, "Approach or go, but make up your mind."

He heard a quiet gasp, or sob, and then the girl—Leyala— appeared beside one of the palm trees. Like Jadin, she had her head bowed in reverence, which annoyed Atan because it meant he couldn't see her face. She wore a veil of copper silk beaded throughout with gold and aquamarine, which meant he also couldn't see her hair. But she was dressed alluringly in a scant topaz robe that was more sheer than opaque, which meant he could see more of her body than he intended. The way she held her arms, one hand pressed to her lips, the other wrapped tight around her chest, whispered shame to be seen so plainly.

He gritted his teeth and looked back at his hand in the water. He would have to talk to Jadin about his assumptions—and his presumption. Just because Atan wanted to see the girl didn't mean he wanted her brought in like an object for him to enjoy and then cast aside. After a moment, he stood without a word and moved past her, heading for his bedchamber. He could hear her trailing after him, hesitant. Fear practically radiated off of her.

She froze beside the latticed ivory screen, in a slant of sunlight slipping through his open window. "Splendor..." she murmured. "Please..."

Her voice was soft, and light, and it would have been lovely if it hadn't been shaking so badly. Atan swept his embroidered copper caftan from the foot of his bed and shook it out. Then, approaching the girl, he draped it wordlessly over her shoulders. She startled and lifted her head, and Atan couldn't resist a small smile. So, she was *that* girl, and now he recalled why he had told Jadin he wanted to know more about her. Whatever Jadin's opinions on the matter, the girl wasn't exceptionally stunning, but she had sapphire-sky eyes that were startlingly bright against the rich darkness of her skin. In a world of golden-eyed Aetherials, she was a rarity.

He stepped past her and returned to his oasis. This time she followed him more quickly.

"Thank you, Splendor," she whispered, as he resumed his spot on the edge of the fountain. "When your servant came to fetch me, and dressed me like this, I was so afraid..."

She cut off all at once, as though the magnitude of her impertinence had suddenly dawned on her. Speaking without invitation to a royal could be an executable offense, but Atan wasn't in the mood for executions at the moment. They were just as dull and pointless as everything else.

"I saw you at the Games, yesterday," Atan said, glossing over everything she had said. He didn't look at her as he spoke, but kept his gaze on the ripples of light moving over the blue and copper mosaic in the fountain's basin.

"Yes, Splendor," Leyala said.

She had stopped beside the palm tree again, waiting for his invitation to come closer. Idly he toyed with the thought of flouting all rules of etiquette and asking her to sit beside him, but the idea gave him no pleasure. Though he would never admit it to anyone, a lifetime of being held aloof from society had left him uncomfortable with people in general. And the way most of them fawned over him, and made obeisance, obsequious and simpering as dogs, was enough to curdle his blood.

He deserved their reverence, certainly. He just preferred them to pay it where he didn't have to see it.

But the silence was festering, so finally he said, "Where are you from?"

"I...beg your pardon?"

He looked at her, at last. With his silk robe held tight around her, she carried herself a little more comfortably, but she still jerked her gaze away from his as soon as their eyes met. He didn't repeat himself. She'd heard him plainly enough, and Atan loathed repeating himself almost as much as he loathed being bored.

When she realized he wasn't going to ask again, she shifted her weight from one hip to the other and, probably without meaning to, lifted an edge of the caftan to worry against her lips. It was a curious self-conscious gesture that Atan found annoyingly attractive.

"I'm from the East, Splendor," she said, softly. "From Kurana."

Atan snorted. It figured she was from Kurana, the only province in Pyria that had ever risen up in civil war against the Star. That had been before his time, which meant it was also likely before Leyala's time. Still, it was odd to find an Easterner in the capital city; as a rule, they tended to keep to themselves. The corner of his mind that was desperate for an end to the numbing boredom wondered if perhaps she was a spy. Maybe the self-conscious shyness was just an act, meant to lower his guard. Perhaps she was an assassin, and he had just invited her into his chambers...

He shook his head. Leyala was as far from an assassin as anyone he could imagine, even if it were possible for him to be assassinated. Still, he couldn't resist a little jab at her heritage.

"If you're here to stir up a revolt, can you at least wait until after dinner?"

She dropped to her knees, letting go of the caftan to bring her hands up in a gesture of appeal, or prayer. "Splendor, I am not!"

He winced, and stifled a sigh. Damn it. He'd meant to make her laugh, not to upset her so profoundly.

"What a shame," he thought—out loud.

"A shame?" she echoed, lifting her chin just a fraction.

The caftan lay in a rumpled heap around her knees. Atan glanced at her, and, without meaning to, looked just long enough that she remembered what she was wearing. She snatched the robe up around her shoulders again, and Atan turned his head so she wouldn't see the amused smile that flashed, unbidden, across his face.

"This damn peace has lasted too long," he muttered.

She rose, cautiously, to her feet. "The peace? You mean the Truce with Nyfalla? You don't honestly mean—"

Again she cut herself off, and this time Atan felt annoyed by her deference. He stood and approached her. At his full height, he was over a head taller than her—Pyrion royalty were always taller than the rest of their kind, and she was no taller than most women. To her credit, she didn't shrink back from him as he stopped in front of her, and for once her blue eyes held his steadily.

For the space of a few seconds, anyway. Then, remembering herself, she broke her gaze from his with a reverent bow of her head. Atan imagined, just for a moment, putting his fingers under her chin and tilting her head back, encouraging her to look at him again…but it was pointless. The only time he could recall touching anyone was in the throes of combat, and he could barely remember what that felt like. It was a lifetime ago. Five lifetimes ago. He couldn't recall.

He could remember the feel of another person's touch even less. It didn't help that his person was sacred; for anyone to touch him without his permission was grounds for immediate execution. A smile, or a grimace, touched his lips as he remembered—Stelyos had grabbed hold of him at the Games to keep him from falling, after he'd used his *ankamis* to save the fallen combatant. Atan wondered briefly if he ought to punish the Captain, but it seemed a foolish triviality. He shook his head to unseat the troublesome thought, and found Leyala studying him curiously.

"You're not like most people I know," he told her.

Feeling suddenly uncomfortable standing so close to her, he moved past her again, folding one hand behind his back as he walked. He returned to his balcony and found the tiger reclining elegantly, propped up on one elbow in the same spot where it had been sleeping before. Leyala ventured onto the balcony a moment later, standing at the very farthest end of it, at the most respectful distance she could manage while still being able to see into the menagerie.

"I've never seen—"

Atan growled in impatience. "If you want to speak, just speak. I'm not in the mood to execute anyone right now, but I might change my mind if you keep doing that."

Her lovely complexion paled, her fear spiking just enough

that her inner light sparkled out. All Pyrions—Pyrions who weren't royalty, anyway—usually kept their light veiled, but in times of high emotion, it shone out unintentionally. Atan regarded his own hands, resting on the marble balustrade. He was used to seeing the shimmer of his dark skin, like sunlight on goldstone. He wondered suddenly what it looked like to other Pyrions. If that was why they kept their heads bowed in his presence. Seeing Leyala's radiance, he wished— irrationally—that everyone might wear their light outwardly like he did. Hers was one of the most beautiful things he had ever seen.

He just wished it wasn't fear of him that caused it.

She stood for a few moments with her hands in fists on the balustrade, head bent. Then she turned to face him. "What do you want from me, Splendor?"

He held her gaze, wordless, testing her. She lasted longer than he expected this time, but eventually, inevitably, she lowered her eyes again.

"Nothing," he said. "I wanted nothing from you. I just hoped you would be different."

Her lips puckered in a faint frown. "Am I?"

"Yes," he said. He turned his attention back to the tiger, feeling the heaviness settle over him again. He didn't know what to do with someone who was different. He didn't know what to do with people in general, except ignore them. "You may go."

She stood frozen, staring at him—he could feel the weight of her gaze on him, though he kept his own attention focused on the tiger.

After a moment he straightened and said, "Leave me now, or I will have my guards escort you out."

She was beside him before he realized she had moved, the caftan left in a heap on the far side of the balcony. One of her long-fingered hands reached up to touch his face. He stiffened instinctively, but didn't draw back as her hand slid behind his neck, beneath the long coils of his hair, to pull his head down toward hers.

"Was I not different enough?" she whispered against his ear, her voice suddenly sultry.

A brief pressure flared under his ribs, then Leyala released him and took one step back. He regarded her in surprise, his gaze straying from her face to the silver knife gripped, shaking, in her hand.

"Where in hell-shadow were you carrying *that*?" he asked, too bewildered to say anything else.

She faltered, her light shimmering again, and she took a half step back like she meant to run.

"What…" she stammered. "Why aren't you…"

Atan rolled his eyes as he put a hand to his side, feeling over the puncture where she had stabbed him. It was already healing; the knife was plain silver, so there wasn't even any ichor on his robe, but the golden silk had a two inch tear in it.

"Damn it all," he said. "You put a hole in it. They just finished embroidering it yesterday, you know." He eyed her sidelong and shook his head. "Sometimes I hate being right," he muttered. "I honestly didn't want to execute you. But you truly thought that slab of metal would hurt me? I am the Splendor, girl."

She stared at the blade in her hand as if it had intentionally betrayed her. With her eyes reddened by tears, her blue irises were more striking than ever. Such a pity.

Atan heaved a weary sigh, then shouted, "Guards!"

He could have diminished her himself, of course. It wouldn't even have been difficult. But she was likely just a pawn in a game she didn't understand, and somehow, that made him reluctant to sever her from their Aether. Capital punishment would be more merciful. At least that way, she could return to the Aether and find some peace.

Barely a moment later, four guards came running into his chamber, their armored feet clashing on the tiled floor. Atan didn't need to make any accusations; Leyala was still standing frozen with the useless knife poised between them. Two of the guards seized her immediately, wrestling the blade from her fingers. One of them caught its edge on his thumb and hissed in pain. Atan flicked a glance at him, then at the golden ichor dripping down to stain his white marble balcony. With another frustrated sigh, he held out his hand and let a little of his *ankamis* flow out through his fingers, closing the gash and mending the pain.

The guard was too professional to stop what he was doing to thank him, but he bowed his head briefly in Atan's direction before he and the other guard marched the girl from his chambers.

"I suppose you should take Jadin too," Atan said reluctantly to the remaining guards, who were staring at him in open awe. "He let her approach me with a knife." He sighed and turned back to watch the tiger, asleep again on the sun-soaked stone. "A damn shame. I was just starting to like him."

THERREI LEFT THE TENEMENT HOUSE at the dawn of Ganrashin, the shadows of night only just creeping away into the alleys and dark corners of the city. The air hung thick with the smell of salt and smoke, the wind whipping up erratically to sting her eyes and cheeks. Eastward the pocked and broken street sloped down toward the rocky shore, disappearing into the silver-blue sea. The sun, just creeping over the ocean's rim, turned the retreating night clouds into a brilliant veil of gold, a flame of cold glory shining off the jittering sea.

She paused a moment to draw a deep breath, and smiled.

The second tolling of the Laysons' bells shattered her reverie. She dropped her canvas bag to pull on her coat, remembering the morning chill with a sudden shiver.

"Therrei!" Sera suddenly shouted from somewhere inside the tenement house. "Therrei, your rent or I'll have Garm throw your things on the street!"

Grimacing, Therrei leaned back through the doorway. "But I don't get paid until tomorrow!" she cried, despairing. Sera knew what day it was—how could she even ask such a thing? "I'll pay you then."

She prayed that it was the truth. Gavin typically paid his workers on time, but she had never counted on it. If he was late...Sera wouldn't *really* throw her out on the street, would she? Therrei had been a good tenant for the last two years—longer than she'd ever lived anywhere. Maybe she'd been late to pay on one or two occasions, but no more than anyone else. And at least she was clean, and quiet. And sober. Unlike Garm.

Therrei shook her head in frustration and focused on buttoning up her wool coat. Pulling up her hood against a gust of wind, she allowed herself one extra moment to watch the beauty of the sunrise unfolding at the edge of the sea.

Then, for no reason at all, she flinched as if someone had struck her.

Desperately she tried to identify the strange sensation creeping over her. It almost felt like being watched—but not quite. It was more like...a sudden bond of shared experience, but that made even less sense. She swept a gaze over the street. Only a few people stood anywhere near her, and all of them ignored her as they hurried on their way. The windows opposite her were dark and empty. The rooftops...

She frowned. The roof of the old hostel across from her was bare but for a few grey gulls roosting on the weather vane, fat from cold, feathers blown all askew by the wind. But somehow...somehow the shadows past the chimney seemed darker, richer than usual. And, pulsing from that spot like new blood, she could almost feel a longing. A wistful sorrow. Regret.

Pain flared through her hands. She clutched her fingers into fists, nails biting flesh as if she could will away the prickling heat, but the hurt was real. The streets almost empty around her, and yet she could feel someone's anguish in the palms of her hands as if he were standing next to her…whoever *he* was. The heat grew more intense, more insistent, until finally she grabbed her bag and darted up the street.

Running away, again, she rebuked herself. *Light and Shadow, how I hate it. I hate it.*

Nearly half an hour later she plowed into the milling throngs in the market square, which was already a tempest of activity even at the very dawn of Ganrashin. Merchants hurried to unveil their booths as the first shoppers began to arrive, while a curious harmony of aromas wove through the chilly air from the food vendors' carts. No moving vehicles—mechanical or otherwise—were allowed within the market, but the streets were crammed with pedestrians, mangy dogs, and mangier urchins looking for handouts or inattentive marks.

Therrei forced her way through the crowd, fighting against the current of humanity, and finally escaped into open air beyond the outermost ring of merchants' stalls. She was exhausted, half-numb from cold, and shaken. Somehow the heat kept surging through her palms, as if the person whose pain she'd felt were still somewhere near her. The idea that someone could have followed her so closely through the crowd was preposterous, though—so preposterous that it actually dragged Therrei to a halt in the middle of the street.

What am I even thinking? Maybe I'm imagining it. Maybe I've always imagined it. As if…as if anyone could really feel someone else's pain. As if it could be me.

Her gaze drifted farther down the main thoroughfare, toward the long iron fence and ornate gate that divided the

Hospice of the Star from the rest of the city. A pair of healers, smartly dressed in their tan and ocean-blue uniforms, stepped through the gate as she watched and made their way into the Markets, laughing as they chatted quietly together. As she watched them, some little pang like envy, or longing, bit at her heart. Then, without consciously making the decision, she began moving toward the Hospice, a fish drawn to a lure.

She was standing before the gate before she managed to stop and consider what she was doing.

Behind her, a voice asked, "Can I help you?"

She jumped and turned to find two men watching her curiously, both garbed as healers. One, a dark-skinned man from Kalimay, wore an embroidered band of white and golden ribbon around the hem of his jacket, an adornment Therrei had never seen before. The other man was rounder in the middle, with heavy, pocked jowls and a marked look of disdain in his pale eyes.

"I'm sorry," Therrei said, dipping her head in courtesy as she backed away from the gate. "I'm in your way."

"Not at all," the Kaliman said. He was the one who had addressed her first, she realized, recognizing the warm, rolling lilt of his voice. "We were at the Temple, going now to the Markets. But you were staring so forlornly at the gate I had to stop."

Therrei smiled in spite of herself, but when she couldn't find her voice to reply, the healer took a step closer to her.

"Are you well? You're trembling."

She clenched and relaxed her hands. "I wanted to speak to someone," she managed. "A healer."

The Kaliman lifted his hands, a broad smile flitting over his face. "You're in luck." He seemed to sense her hesitation, because he scanned the milling crowd briefly before lifting a hand toward the narrow pedestrian door beside the gate. "Inside, perhaps?"

She nodded her thanks and waited for him to open the door—it was locked, but the man had a key. With a vague wave of his hand, he beckoned her to follow him inside the cloister. The other man, to her dissatisfaction, entered in close on her heels. Near the center of the courtyard, amidst raised stone flower beds and urns cradling fruit trees, green even in the late month, the Kaliman healer sat down on a marble bench and patted the spot beside him. As Therrei sat, the other healer moved a little to the side, arms folded, displeasure deepening the lines around his eyes.

"Now then," the Kaliman said. "What seems to be troubling you? My name is Elyon Bayn, by the way. I'm the Master Healer of the Hospice, but don't let that alarm you. I'm just an old healer at heart."

The other man smirked faintly and turned his head to stare out over the gardens.

For a moment Therrei watched him, then with a sigh she turned to Master Bayn and said, "It's nothing wrong with me. At least—I don't think it is."

"Then why are you troubling the Master Healer?" the large man said.

Therrei frowned up at him, but Bayn only lifted a hand to dismiss his indignation. "Don't mind him. Speak to me as if he isn't even here."

"Can he...*not* be here?" Therrei whispered. "I'd rather speak to you alone."

Bayn gave her a kind smile, kinder than any she'd received of late, and said, "He will stay. But I promise you—" and he gave the rotund man a dangerous glare—"he will not interrupt again."

Therrei shifted her weight on the cold bench. The sun was just climbing high enough to thaw some of the frost from the air, but in the shadow of the white-stone Hospice, the air was still quite chilly. Therrei's hands should have been numb, but instead they prickled with a subtle heat—picking up some trace pain from one of the two men. She just wasn't sure which...or if she was only imagining it.

"I feel things," she said after a moment.

Bayn frowned; apparently her statement was ambiguous enough to be unintelligible.

She let out a sharp breath and waved a hand between them, as if that helped explain anything. "I can feel it when other people are in pain," she said. "In my hands. In...in my spirit."

"What do you mean, *feel* things?" Bayn asked, gently.

"My hands turn hot. When I'm Seaming someone—that's what I call it, anyway—but when I Seam them, it's like I'm stitching their soul into my own. If they have a pain in their arm, I feel a pain in my arm. If they have a headache, I have a headache. The closer they are to me, the more intensely I feel it. If they touch me I can't escape it. What does it mean?"

Bayn watched her quietly, offering no reaction to her words the whole time she spoke. When she fell silent, he went on studying until she fidgeted under the weight of his stare.

"You feel what other people feel," he said, without inflection.

"Yes, sir."

"And what," he said, "do you imagine I could do for you?"

Therrei's shoulders slumped and she bowed her head. "Nothing, sir. I don't imagine it's anything you could heal. But I've always wanted..."

She bit her tongue, hard, and forced herself to embrace the silence.

It's pointless, she told herself. *It's a stupid idea. Don't even bother asking.*

"Wanted what?"

"To help," she said, barely whispering. "I want to be a healer."

The larger man made some noise of disgust or contempt, but Bayn only shot him a dark glare over his shoulder before turning back to Therrei. For one long moment he studied her intently, then, with a small shake of his head, he got to his feet and ushered her toward the gate ahead of him.

"Let me consider your claim," he said as they neared the street. "But I make no promises."

"Of course not," said Therrei, with a forced lightness she did not believe.

Bayn opened the gate and Therrei, stepping out onto the street, turned back to bid them farewell. As she did, she caught a pointed look pass between the two men that doused whatever feeble ember of hope remained in her heart.

"I'm sorry to have wasted your time," she murmured, and without waiting for their reply, she let the current of townsfolk sweep her toward the Markets, away from the Hospice.

But no matter how carefully she tried to blend into the crowd, the prickle-cold feeling of being watched plagued her steps the rest of the day.

IN THE SHADOW OF ONE of the rust-stained factory buildings, under a lowering sky that threatened rain, two men watched the throng swirl through the Markets.

"Do you suppose it's true?" the older man asked.

The other, a smaller man, bald-headed, cold and remote as the sea, said, "I cannot say for certain. Are you confident in your sources? They were absolutely sure of what the girl said?"

The large man nodded, scowling as he stared into the crowd. "I thought *she* promised you—"

"Don't speak to me about that woman," the other said, savagely.

"How could she have thwarted you?"

He spun and jabbed a finger at the bigger man's throat, but made no more threat than that. "I need you to follow this. Find out if the girl is telling the truth." With one more glance at the Markets, he shook his head and drew up the hood of his coat. "Damn it all. I'd curse that woman to the underbelly of Vesper if she weren't already dead."

Bonus Content

The World of Chaos Lies

Chaos Lies takes place in what is best described as a multi-dimensional cosmos. The Aethers do not occupy a physical place in relation to the human world, but they are in fact physical places to the Aetherials who live there. However, it can be helpful to visualize the Aethers as forming a shell that surrounds the human world, a barrier between the mortal world and the Outer Night. The human world, on the other hand, is the barrier, or Wall, between all realms and Chaos in his cage.

The Cosmos

Outer Night: The First, the primordial darkness. What came before and will outlast all. Pure and enduring, a force of stability and simplicity, and the opposite in every way to Chaos.

Nyfalla: The Aether of Shadow. Shadow has an affinity to the Outer Night, but is not itself pure darkness. Nyfalla is a cold, rugged, unforgiving place, with vast moors, jagged rocks, glaciers, and a vibrant night sky where the Ankathe, or what we would call the Borealis, constantly shines. Nyfalla is ruled by a *Skaed*.

Nyfallans can incarnate in the mortal world in darkness and deep shadow, but are burned by light. Aetherials of Shadow live at night and sleep during the day. They are characterized by pale skin, grey to silver eyes, and dark hair that has a silver iridescence. They favor a brutal honesty in their words, but also excel in stealth and clandestine arts.

Pyria: The Aether of Light. Light has a natural repulsion from Outer Night, but they exist in a necessary, though tenuous, balance. Pyria is a bright, lush place, with verdant tropical oases among sprawling red hills and a warm, languid climate. At night the brilliant blue sky shifts to an amber warmth, never fully dark. Pyria is ruled by the Star, and secondarily by his heir, the Splendor.

Pyrians can incarnate in the mortal world in daylight and bright light, but are burned by darkness. Like mortals, they live by day and sleep at night. They have dark skin and black hair, and most Pyrians have golden eyes, though some have blue eyes. They are generally mellow and generous unless provoked, but see no issue with bending the truth to suit their needs.

The *Loryan*: The liminal space between the Aethers and the mortal world. It is the portal realm which binds their dimensions. It is a nebulous place where distance is fluid and, with a little practice, easily manipulated.

Arkastel: The mortal realm. This is the world where humans live. Trapped at the heart of the world is Chaos, bound in a cage and kept asleep by the power of the Aethers. Taris is the capital city of the Vanethan Empire. Mystics, scholars, and theomancers call it the Conduit, because Taris is more closely connected both to Chaos and the Aethers than anywhere else in the world.

The Lord Prince, who is Emperor of Vaneth, maintains a treaty with the princes of Light and Shadow. The Aetherials patrol the streets of Taris watching for fissures in Chaos's cage, and exterminating any shards of Chaos that esape. What, exactly, the Aetherials receive in return is not well understood—even by the theomancers of the High Fane themselves.

The Characters

The Fane

Ingmar vel Karda: Acolyte of the Fane.
Palimo: Acolyte of the Fane; abandons his vows.
Sister Resida: Theomancer; High Cleric and Invoker
Brother Garrim: Theomancer; Magister of ritual and Aetherial lore.
Brother Havlor: Theomancer; Magister of history

Nyfalla

Skaed **Morayn:** Prince of Nyfalla; Emery's best friend
Trelian: Captain of the Hauskell Guard

Emery: Captain in the Nyfallan Guard
Reman: One of Emery's soldiers; killed in Taris
Brana: Captain in the Nyfallan Guard; close friend of Emery's
Amura: Another Captain in the Nyfallan Guard
Kohla: Seeress; Counselor to *Skaed* Morayn

Pyria

Atan: the Splendor; prince of Pyria, heir of the Star
Jadin: Atan's valet
Stelyos: the Captain of Atan's bodyguard
Leyala: a Pyrion from the eastern province of Kurana

Taris

Therrei tol Dana: sweep in a textile mill; has empathic powers
Dessa: Therrei's best friend
Traven: patron of Therrei's favorite tavern; fear-mongerer
Sera: landlady of Therrei's tenement house
Garm: tenant in Sera's lodging; habitual drunkard
Gavin: Therrei's foreman
Elyon Bayn: Master Healer of the Hospice of the Star

The Words

Theomancer: cleric of the High Fane
High Fane: temple devoted to the worship of the Aetherials
Skaed: Lord or prince (of Nyfalla)
Ankathe: the Borealis
Hauskell: the *Skaed* of Nyfalla's fortress and mead hall

Makhdem: the Splendor's blade of judgment, capable of severing a Pyrion from the Aether of Light for eternity

Ankamis: the innate healing power belonging to the Star and his Splendor; a channeling of the Aether of Light

Loryan: the liminal space binding the Aethers and mortal world together

Ginnregin: the innate, prophetic Sight belonging to the *Skaed* of Nyfalla; a channeling of the Aether of Shadow.

Episode 2:
SNEAK PEEK

ARKASTEL — CITY OF TARIS

25 YEARS AGO

I N THE LATE AFTERNOON HOUR, THE SUN SUMMER-HIGH AND unyielding, the Fane's library was a prism of rich golden light and hollow shadows. The silence was sepulchral. Only the occasional whisper of turning pages marred the stillness, as a scattering of clerics and visiting scholars delved into ancient tomes. Ingmar perched on a hard bench across the wide study table from Brother Garrim—Garrim bent over a thick book, sunlight glinting on the silver streaks in his dark hair, Ingmar frowning at a sheaf of papers he was supposed to be copying. His pen had drifted in meaningless circles over the parchment for at least an hour, but Garrim, single-minded, lost in his own work, had not even noticed.

"Will she live forever, in Nyfalla?" asked Ingmar, staring pensively at Brother Garrim.

The older cleric startled and peered at the acolyte over

the top of his grease-smudged spectacles. Ingmar wasn't surprised—neither of them had spoken a word all morning. Garrim had likely forgotten about his presence long ago.

"What—who?" the cleric asked, scowling. "The girl? The oblation for the *Skaed*?"

Ingmar only nodded.

"Boy, are you still thinking about that? That was six months ago." When Ingmar didn't reply, Garrim sighed and closed his book, and removed the spectacles from his nose. "We don't actually know what happens to them when they reach the Aether. Can mortals survive outside our realm? We know the Aetherials can survive here in our world—so long as they stay in their proper element—but what is the proper element for a mortal in an Aetherial realm? How I long to question one of them and find out!"

"How many others have there been?"

Garrim did not answer for a long time. "I know of two in my lifetime. One offering to the Star of Pyria, when I was quite young, and this one to the *Skaed*."

Ingmar frowned, fiddling with the thin, script-heavy paper in front of him. "The Nyfallan said she was shadow-marked. What did that mean?"

"It means that some of their *Skaed*'s power—his *ginnregin*—slipped through the cracks of the cosmos, so to speak, and touched her soul. So by rights she belongs to him. The same was true of Erana. She was touched by the Star's power, and so we offered her to him."

"What power?"

Garrim eyed him patiently. "She could heal the sick with

just her touch. There are rumors her powers were more… *varied* than that, but I don't know if I put any stock in those stories. She was a founding member of our Hospice, at any rate, and served there until she was given to Pyria."

Ingmar pondered that, working through the implications. If this Erana had been able to heal the sick without medicine, what power did the shadow-marked girl have? He thought of the Nyfallan, reducing Sister Resida to a vacuous nothingness with a single gesture. Resida had died a few days later. No one said how; in the scarred corners of his heart, Ingmar guessed the other clerics had killed her to end her suffering.

"Why would we send them away?" he asked at last. "Wouldn't it be better to have people with such incredible powers here to help us? People who are…*people*." He paused, then finished, bitterly, "Not Aetherials. Not capricious like Aetherials."

Garrim steepled his hands beneath his chin and stared a long while at his acolyte. "Perhaps. But tell me what you think. What would happen to the soul of a human who wielded such power for a lifetime? Power has a habit of changing those who embrace it. And power like *that*? Some argue that even a person as kind and good as Erana would be unable to withstand the lure of using it outside proper boundaries. That is why the Fane sees the manifestation of these Aether-touched souls as an omen, a portent of inevitable disaster if left unchecked. So they deem it better to send them to the Aethers where, even with such great gifts, they are still nothing compared to the rulers from whom their power comes. The Aethers can *contain* them."

"Contain them?" Ingmar echoed, but Garrim didn't answer.

Ingmar slouched on the bench, head in his hands, vexed and dissatisfied. If the power of Aetherial rulers was so terrible, so corrupting, then why would the theomancers of the Fane devote themselves to their worship? From what he had seen of the Nyfallan emissary, he would much rather deal with a human with extraordinary power than an Aetherial with the same power. Humans, at least, could be reasoned with. And if not…they could be killed. As far as he had ever learned, Aetherials could not be killed by anything except the limits of their own nature.

He sighed and gathered up his papers. "I'm done for today, Brother," he said. "I'll finish these tomorrow."

Garrim, still mired in thought, simply waved a hand in acknowledgement. After he'd returned his papers to their proper case, Ingmar left the library and stepped out into the sweating afternoon. With a few hours yet until dinner, he had a rare span of time all to himself, unfettered by the Fane's rigid schedule. He could see no one else but the gardener, but the man was busy grappling with the overzealous hedges near the refectory and didn't see Ingmar lingering on the path. The Faneguard would be on patrol elsewhere on the property, and the two guards who stood ceremonial watch at the Temple's doors were too far away to see him. Steeling his resolve, Ingmar ducked through the western gate and onto the main street of Arkastel.

Away from the humid shade of the Fane's overgrown gardens, the air felt pleasanter, sun-soaked and golden, teasing the coming evening. Ingmar dodged a carriage headed toward the palace and let a small river of people sweep him up in its eddies. They tugged him down toward the market district where the usual small crowd had gathered among the booths and stands, shopping for last-minute essentials before the market closed down for the evening.

Ingmar wandered without purpose among the colorfully-draped booths. His acolyte's robe garnered him some reverence among the merchants; one offered him a ripe pear, and another, a merchant of Kalimay, bowed as she gave him a packet of toasted whitenut shavings. He was just cleaning the pear's honey-sweet juice from his fingers when he heard someone hiss his name.

Startled, he turned and spotted Palimo crouching in an alley behind the whitenut merchant's booth. Ingmar stifled a scowl. An uncharitable corner of his heart had hoped the other boy would be scrawny, filthy, and half wild from his life away from the Fane. But Palimo looked healthier than ever… and worse than that, he actually looked *happy*. As Ingmar wandered toward him, Palimo gave him a broad, genuine grin that only slightly mollified Ingmar's sour mood.

"Ingmar! It's good to see you!" he said, grabbing Ingmar in a fierce hug.

Ingmar tolerated him a moment before brushing the other boy off. "Why are you whispering?"

Palimo shrugged and shook his head at the same time, still smiling. "Felt like I should. But you! What are you doing in the market? Finally thinking of running away?"

"I don't run away," Ingmar said with a glower.

"Well, I did, and I don't regret it for a moment." Palimo winked impishly at him. "I do as like, when I like, and eat whatever the hell I want on whatever day I want to eat it. Also, people know I used to serve the Fane. *Eka*, I've been telling them all what a bunch of nonsense it was."

Ingmar blinked, stunned. "You've been *what?*"

"It was your idea, remember? You said instead of telling people the Aetherials are monsters, we should tell them they don't exist. So that's what I've been doing." He folded his hands prayerfully before him. With the sun setting behind him, his tawny hair framed his face like a golden glow. "I was an acolyte of the Fane. I *know* what I'm talking about, of course. And look at me—who would ever imagine I was lying?"

Ingmar snorted and turned away, letting his gaze drift over the dwindling crowd. In the deepening shadows, more and more people began to hurry homeward with their purchases.

"How can they tolerate the curfew one moment and believe what you're saying about the Aetherials the next? Don't they remember what the Nyfallans were doing to them, before?"

"Rumors," said Palimo, shrugging. "Hearsay."

Ingmar shuddered, remembering the cruel-eyed Nyfallan, hearing the ice in his voice as he said those very words.

"You give people too much credit, Ingmar. It's easier not to believe at all…"

Can't wait for more? Grab episode 2 today!

Did you enjoy the first episode?

Please consider leaving a review on your favorite site to let others know what you think!

Reviews are incredibly valuable to all authors, especially indie authors...but we also just love to hear from you!

Don't miss any of the latest news and updates...
Scan here to sign up for my email newsletter!

Get sneak peeks at my WIPs, bonus scenes, deleted scenes, artwork, and much more...but no spam!

Just for signing up you get a free copy of my Writers of the Future semifinalist short story, *The Silence Between*.

Acknowledgments

There are so many people I have to thank for making me believe in this project, and encouraging me to dare to try something new. James Artimus Owen, Marie Whittaker, and Todd Fahnestock — you are all treasures. Your advice, support and encouragement have been priceless. Special thanks also go to Geni, Cecilia, and my ARC team for the enthusiasm and invaluable feedback. I would still be sitting on this project without you.

About the Author

J. Leigh Bralick is the author of the Lost Road Chronicles, a YA fantasy, and Chaos Lies Beneath the Night, a gaslamp serial fantasy, not counting the myriad other novels she swears she will finish at some point. She hoards learning and new experiences like a dragon and would never turn down the opportunity to visit a new place. After spending a year in the beautiful state of Montana, she is back in her home state of Texas where she divides her time between working as an ER nurse, writing, and pursuing half a dozen other semi-related projects.

She and her husband are happily owned by three crazy dogs who think they're humans, a conure who thinks he's a bat, two gas station goldfish that won't die (long story), four chickens bent on world domination, and a danger noodle with no teeth.

Also by J. Leigh Bralick

THE LOST ROAD CHRONICLES

Down a Lost Road (Lost Road Chronicles #1)
Subverter (Lost Road Chronicles #2)
Prism (Lost Road Chronicles #3)
Down a Lost Road: Special Extended Edition

THE MADNESS METHOD

The Madness Project (Madness Method #1)
A Dark So Deep (Madness Method #2)
A Sea Like Glass (Madness Method #3)
The Hollow King (Madness Method #4 - coming soon!)
Untitled (madness Method #5 - coming later!)

SHORT STORIES

Of Smoke and Wind (Fantasy)
The Silence Between (Sci-Fi)